A Touch of Love

❧ GLENNA ❧ FINLEY

When eyes meet far off,
our sense is such that—
we feel the tenderest touch.

—Dryden

A SIGNET BOOK

NEW AMERICAN LIBRARY

NAL BOOKS ARE AVAILABLE AT QUANTITY DISCOUNTS
WHEN USED TO PROMOTE PRODUCTS OR SERVICES.
FOR INFORMATION PLEASE WRITE TO PREMIUM MARKETING DIVISION,
NEW AMERICAN LIBRARY, 1633 BROADWAY,
NEW YORK, NEW YORK 10019.

SIGNET, SIGNET CLASSIC, MENTOR, PLUME, MERIDIAN and NAL BOOKS are published by New American Library, 1633 Broadway, New York, New York 10019

First Printing, May, 1985

1 2 3 4 5 6 7 8 9

PRINTED IN THE UNITED STATES OF AMERICA

LOVE'S PRETENDERS ❧

The sound of footsteps made Kent stiffen, and before Barbara knew it, he yanked her into a close embrace, his face hidden from the intruder. "What do you think . . ." began Barbara—but Kent's mouth came down to cover hers in a brusque, long kiss that had Barbara hanging onto his shoulders as her mind whirled and she began to respond. Suddenly, he released her as abruptly as he had reached for her.

"Quiet!" he whispered, as Barbara realized he was making sure the unexpected visitor had vanished altogether. "O.K.," he breathed, relaxing. "He's gone for now, but you can bet our friend is after a lot more than a glimpse of two lovers locked in a kiss."

"I don't appreciate being dragged into your mysterious games," Barbara said firmly. But she had to admit—his kiss had turned her into a willing player. . . .

SIGNET Romances by Glenna Finley

～§ 1 §～

The center of London was one solid sea of people, Barbara Stratton decided when she stared out of her taxi window that sunny May morning.

Old people, young ones, career types, and tourists—they overflowed the sidewalks to spill onto the busy streets and made her wonder why she'd spent a small fortune to join the crowd. As the driver turned toward St. James Square, she felt only relief that she was finally approaching a place where she could close her eyes in privacy—a luxury that she'd been denied too long.

At that moment, she would have told anyone who'd listen that international travel was an endurance contest rather than the effortless wafting of bodies around the globe promised by television commercials.

Some twenty-three hours before when she'd started from California on the first leg of our journey, she'd been filled with joie de vivre—or at least as much joie de vivre as anyone could feel after getting up at four A.M. to start for the airport. Breakfast aboard the transcontinental flight had revived her somewhat and even the announcement that they'd forgotten to put a movie aboard didn't particularly faze her. It *was* a little disconcerting to be stuck in a holding pattern between Canada and Florida for an hour before landing in New York. When she eventually deplaned at JFK in a driving rain, her last twinge of enthusiasm had disappeared along with the blue sky. The two hours before her London connection went by in a blur of bodies propped around the waiting room and she trailed onto the plane in early evening feeling as if she'd come through light years from another world.

Modern technology suffered another blow when the plummy-voiced New York captain announced there was a "spot of mechanical trouble, but it shouldn't delay us unduly on our trip across the Atlantic." He sounded less cheerful an hour later when he announced that although the mechanical trouble was solved, one runway at the airport was closed for maintenance. As a result, they were behind twenty-six other airplanes waiting for takeoff. The concerted groan from his passengers must have been heard in Miami, and Barbara rested her head against the side of the airplane, wondering why in hell her ancestors had ever ventured west of the Appalachians in the first place.

Once they finally took off, there were six-and-a-half hours more to get through before the plane settled with a jarring thump at Heathrow—showing that the pilot's buoyant spirits had evaporated by then, too.

The first really cheerful person Barbara saw after she staggered off the plane was the British Immigration Officer who wanted to know her reason for coming to England.

"To spend money," she advised him tersely.

"That's as good a reason as I've heard all day. Glad to have you with us," he replied, grinning, and handed back her stamped passport.

Her sense of humor surfaced slightly at that and if she hadn't suffered an overpowering urge to go to bed by then, she would have enjoyed the ride from Heathrow to London through intermittent sprinkles of rain, and thin sunshine.

At that moment her taxi jerked to a stop in the narrow Duke of York Street. Her tired face must have spurred the driver's sense of chivalry because he came around to lug her bags up the four steps to the front door of a modest brick building which housed the flat she'd rented before she left home.

Her key to the building was big enough to have been used for King Arthur's castle and when Barbara went into the dim foyer an instant later, she decided the idea wasn't too farfetched. The ancient surroundings could have served as a pied-à-terre in Guinevere's time—if she'd wanted to spend a night in town.

The tenants' mail was scattered haphazardly

on a knee-high counter to her left, but the overhead light was so dim that she needed a candle to decipher the names on the envelopes.

Not that it mattered, since she couldn't expect any mail for a week or so. Her expression clouded slightly at that prospect and then she administered a mental shake. One attractive part of travel was isolation from the familiar, she told herself. What wasn't fun was having to move suitcases that weighed a ton—at least a ton, she decided, shifting hers toward the elevator cubicle.

The lift was of modern vintage, but only big enough to hold three very thin people or one average one and a hefty suitcase. Which meant she'd have to make a second trip to transfer all her belongings.

She pushed the button for the fourth level as the rental agent had instructed—although how flat sixteen came to be on level four was a mystery. The tiny elevator lurched its way upward, finally grinding to a halt at the next to the top floor. Barbara watched the inner gate open and she turned to grasp the handle of her suitcase.

But even as she reached for it, the inner gate slammed shut with brisk efficiency and, before she could reach the button to punch level four again, the elevator was on its way down.

It had barely settled at ground level when the outer door was pulled open and she found herself looking up at a tall, dark-haired man who appeared both surprised and annoyed to find the elevator already occupied.

The frown on his tanned face changed to bland courtesy as he said, "Looks as if you could use some help with that," and removed her suitcase from the elevator.

He set it on the carpet and straightened, frowning again when he saw that she'd stayed determinedly where she was. As if to remind her, he held the inner gate pointedly open and stood waiting.

Barbara took a deep breath and looked at a spot two inches over his shoulder. At any other time, she wouldn't have been so reluctant to meet his gray-eyed glance. Six-foot men on the right side of thirty with thick dark hair, well-tailored clothes, and nice rugged features rated a careful survey—if a woman had any red corpuscles left.

But at that moment, both Barbara's red and white corpuscles felt as if they'd gone into hibernation and all she wanted to do was join them. She said, without any diplomacy at all, "Would you kindly put that suitcase back where you found it." And, when his frown deepened, she added, "I *was* going up—before you took the elevator away from me."

"You mean I . . ." He broke off then, grinning.

"Exactly." Barbara was past the point of seeing anything amusing about it. Or anything else, for that matter. "The suitcase," she reminded him, putting a foot out to hold the gate so the farce couldn't be continued.

"The suitcase," the man repeated and bent down obediently. He managed to keep his voice under control as he cast a glance toward her other piece of luggage still sitting in the middle of the foyer. "What about that one?"

"What about it?" Barbara's tone wasn't encouraging.

"I presume it's yours."

"That's right."

"I just wondered if it's going up or has come down."

She almost said, "What difference does it make?" until she noticed that his shoe was keeping the elevator door open and she was scarcely in a position to take on a full-scale skirmish. "It's going up—eventually. This thing isn't big enough to hold everything."

"Then—allow me," he drawled. "I'll bring it with me. What level are you?"

"Level?" She blinked dazedly up at him.

"Floor. What's the number of your flat?"

"Oh—" Barbara closed her eyes to think. "Sixteen," she managed finally. "It's on the fourth floor."

"Are you sure?"

If she hadn't known better, she would have thought that there was a new quality to his tone. Certainly the lightly disguised amusement had disappeared. She stared at him, but the only thing that really registered was an overpowering tiredness. If the discussion went on much longer, she knew she'd fall asleep standing up in the elevator. It would have to be standing up because there certainly wasn't room to lie down.

She encountered his direct gaze again and realized that he'd repeated his question and was obviously waiting for an answer. "Of course I'm sure," she flared back. "That's what the rental agent told me. Although why it should matter to you—"

"You're right," he cut in before she could finish the sentence. "Just push the button and I'll be right behind you with your other case."

She nodded and scarcely waited for his polished oxford to be removed before she punched the button and lurched upward in the elevator again.

When it stopped at four, she quickly kept the gate open with her elbow as she shoved her suitcase and belongings out onto the landing. No sooner had she emerged herself than the door snapped shut and she heard the elevator descending.

The fourth level landing was almost as dim as the downstairs foyer with three doors that opened onto it. She was just inserting her key into number sixteen when she heard the elevator door open again behind her.

A quick glance over her shoulder showed that her new acquaintance from the lobby had arrived with her other piece of luggage, and she paused with the apartment door just ajar to nod her thanks. "I appreciate your help, but I can manage from here on." She flashed a fleeting smile and concentrated on shoving her first suitcase into the flat, using it to prop the door open as she turned to get the rest of her belongings.

A masculine shoulder loomed up in front of her as she straightened, putting the second bag neatly alongside her other one. "You needn't have bothered," Barbara told him, keeping a smile determinedly on her face as she tried not to sag against the door frame. "Thanks again—it was very kind of you."

With that, she struggled to get both her bags clear and closed the apartment door firmly, leaving her benefactor still standing in the hallway. She shook her head as she dropped her keys onto the tiny foyer table and surveyed herself in the mirror above it. It was strange that he was so persistent—considering that she looked as if she'd been without sleep for three days straight instead of just two. Her light-brown hair was hanging lank and straight around her pale face and her lipstick had disappeared somewhere over Nantucket. She brushed a strand of hair back from her forehead and scowled at the dark smudges under her hazel eyes. It was a wonder that Galahad of the Elevator hadn't run in the opposite direction.

She shrugged out of her topcoat as she moved from the compact hallway into the living room of the flat, casting a quick glance of approval at the pale-yellow divans on either side of the tiny room with its slanted ceiling windows. The bamboo-green color of the carpet was lightened for the walls—giving the interior a cheerful aspect even with the darkening sky and raindrops starting to appear on the windowpanes. The rest of the flat apparently consisted of a kitchenette so narrow that it had to be seen to be believed and a bathroom which fortunately was of normal dimensions. She wandered back to the living room and through another open door which led to the dressing room.

The first thing that met her glance there was the big armoire. She walked automatically toward it to find a hanger for her coat and almost fell flat as she stumbled over a leather suitcase and a nylon duffel bag. "Damn it all to hell," she muttered as she reached down to rub her knee and check if she'd ruined her panty hose. She'd just discovered the beginning of a run when there was a reverberating knock from the front hall. That brought forth a murmured comment from her which, fortunately, fell on an empty room as she limped back to the door.

"You!" she said witheringly as she flung it open and saw the now-familiar masculine figure, apparently set to bang the knocker again. She took a deep breath and said in a measured, ominous cadence, "Look, I don't want to sound unpleasant, but I've just spent the better part of my life getting over here, so I don't feel sociable. All I want to do is find something soft—preferably with a roof over it to keep out the rain . . ."

"That was my idea, too . . ."

". . . so go find somebody else's door or suitcase. Haymarket's full of tour buses with women who'd be tickled pink to have you hanging around." At that point of her tirade, Barbara noticed his rocklike stance on the threshold and she recalled his last comment. "What do you mean—about it being your idea, too?" she got out finally.

"Just that." He jerked a thumb toward the interior of her flat. "Unfortunately, we picked the same pied-à-terre."

"You mean?"

"The same apartment," he said, not bothering to hide his impatience. "Same roof, same plumbing, same rental agent."

Barbara's eyes narrowed as she tried to concentrate. "Then that stuff in the dressing room . . ."

"The leather bag and the duffel?" At her reluctant nod, he added, "Mine. So maybe we could discuss this someplace out of the draft." And then when she still hesitated, he reached in his pocket and extracted a familiar-looking key. "I've been damned decent so far. All I had to do was let myself back in."

Barbara clutched a handful of her hair, trying to hide the terrible realization that what she really wanted to do was clutch his throat . . . firmly and violently until he would stop making noises about his rights to *her* living space. Finally, she stepped back so that he could enter the tiny foyer. "All right—but don't get any mistaken ideas about American women. Some of you British seem to think—"

"British!" he exploded, not letting her finish the sentence. "Hell's bells, I'm not British. What gives you that idea?"

"You sound like it," she insisted stubbornly, her chin outthrust. "At least, sort of."

"Well, I've spent a lot of time here, but if you scratched me, you'd hit Yankee blood straight through." He caught himself to grimace with annoyance. "Although I'm damned if I know what that has to do with anything."

"Well, somebody must be responsible for this fiasco. From what I've seen"—Barbara gestured toward the living room just a step away—"this place is barely big enough for a midget—let alone two average-sized people. So don't get any ideas," she added for good measure.

His eyebrows climbed. "You're not in a position to be issuing ultimatums. To put it bluntly, I was here first."

"I can see that chivalry must have drowned on this edge of the Atlantic." She started toward the telephone at the far end of the nearest settee. "Maybe Mrs. Carling can straighten this out."

He put out an involuntary hand to stop her. "You know Janice?" And when she stared, uncomprehending, "I mean Mrs. Carling."

Barbara nodded as she replied, "Obviously not as well as you do. My acquaintance consists of one long-distance phone call and sending her a check which she promptly cashed. Maybe you can tell me if double-booking is a practice of hers." She brushed a weary hand over her forehead.

"Why don't you sit down before you fall down," he said, gesturing toward the couch. "There's no need to get upset—we'll work it out one way or another."

"It's that one way or another that's upsetting

me," Barbara confessed, perching on the edge of the cushion as he suggested.

"You don't look very comfortable," he pointed out.

"I don't dare relax." She blinked, aware that her eyelids seemed to have taken on a recent coating of sandpaper. "If I did, I wouldn't surface for twelve hours. On the other hand, maybe that's the best idea. You and Mrs. Carling can figure this out while I hold down the fort here."

"You might not like the result," he said, an amused expression softening his features. "Incidentally, I'm Kent Michaels." He paused expectantly.

"Barbara Stratton," she said and then added, "I wish you wouldn't start being nice. It makes it a lot more difficult for me to throw you out."

"Don't give it a thought. Besides, I'm about to let you win the first round. I had a decent sleep here last night and I can bunk in with a friend of mine near Sloane Square for the moment."

"We really should get this settled now . . ."

"Why not wait until tomorrow? After you've had twelve hours sleep, we can go at it hammer and tongs. This way, I'd feel I had to give you a handicap. Only one thing," he added, pausing on his way toward the dressing room to retrieve his belongings.

She looked at him warily. "What did you have in mind?"

"Just that I'd like to leave one bag here—that

way, I won't look as if I'm moving in for the season when I appear on my friend's doorstep." As he saw Barbara start to frown, he added, "Besides, there isn't much chance of getting a taxi in this weather and it's a damn nuisance to wrestle two bags on the underground during rush hours."

Anybody who'd ever traveled on a subway could recognize the logic in that statement, and she nodded reluctantly.

"So now I'll be on my way." He lingered in the front hallway, holding the smaller of his two bags. "There's milk and the makings of breakfast in the kitchen."

"But I can't take your—"

She broke off as he gestured impatiently, saying, "Consider it lend-lease. I'll be in touch," and was out the front door before she could make any other protests.

Barbara thought about following him out to the hall—to insist on having a telephone number or at least a definite time for when he'd be back to retrieve his other belongings. Then she heard the sound of the lift door closing and knew that she'd left it too late.

Which was just as well, she told herself, wondering if she had the strength to plug in the electric kettle on the kitchen counter and make herself a cup of tea. Then she decided that it wasn't really necessary. It made a great deal more sense to pull off the bolster on the couch and root out a blanket and pillow from the armoire in the dressing room. She noted approvingly that Kent Michaels had pushed his suitcase against the wall so that the tiny room didn't resemble an obstacle course any longer. She even gave silent thanks to her unknown landlord because the pillow was goose down rather than ground-up inner tubes and the pale-yellow blanket was fine merino wool.

Why bother to undress? she asked herself as she sank onto the convertible bed and let her eyelids fall. After all, she just needed a short nap— then she'd get up to eat dinner and plan the rest of her evening.

When she next opened her eyes, she stared up into a London sky with only a sliver of moon visible to silhouette the tall buildings of Mayfair. In her sleep-dazed state, it took a while for her to finally remember where she was and still longer to read the luminous digital clock atop the bookcase. She wondered if her stomach were on a time zone all of its own and debated going in the kitchen to try and solve that dilemma. Then she yawned and turned over, deciding that sleep was more important.

It took the first rays of morning sun to awaken her hours later and she stretched luxuriously under her blanket. Unfortunately, a determined knocking on the front door interrupted her pleasant somnolent state and brought her reluctantly upright. She gave a disbelieving gasp as she checked the time again, while searching for her shoes. That quest was fruitless and she noticed in passing that her outfit was not improved by sleeping in it. If the knocking hadn't continued, she would have made a beeline for the bathroom, shedding her clothes on the way. As she went into the hall, she noticed the chain lock which she had forgotten to engage the night before.

Kent Michaels' first words showed that he hadn't forgotten it. "My God, don't you even check to see who's knocking before you open the door?"

"If I had, there wouldn't have been anything left but splinters."

"That's because I've been knocking for the better part of five minutes. I was about to call nine-nine-nine for the emergency squad." His glance didn't miss a thing as it traveled her bedraggled figure. "I gather you just got up."

Barbara looked at him with acute distaste, knowing it didn't take a genius to figure that out. "Do you make a habit of calling at dawn or did you forget something when you moved out?"

"I didn't move out," he said, stepping across the threshold. He took her hand from the knob and then closed the door behind him. "I merely let you move in—for the time being."

"That isn't the way I remember it . . ."

"Well, there's no point in raising our blood pressure over it. What I really came to do was take you out for coffee. There's a place in the next block that even has tolerably good Danish to go with it."

That suggestion did wonders for soothing her indignation. She automatically ran a hand through her untidy hair, wishing to heaven that she'd reached a comb before reaching for the doorknob. "I'll have to change," she said without any appreciable conviction.

"That's all right. I can wait for you." A sheepish expression softened his features. "I forgot to mention that my things are still in the medicine cabinet."

She gestured toward the bathroom. "Then be my guest. I haven't even moved my toothbrush in."

"At least I can shift my belongings onto one shelf until we hold our discussion and it'll be nice to reclaim my toothbrush. You should have seen me using the end of a turkish towel earlier . . ." As he saw the beginning of her smile, he added, "Maybe it was just as well you didn't. I wasn't in a very good mood."

"Apparently we have something else in common," she admitted. "I'm not exactly a 'rise and shine' type myself. Maybe you noticed."

Kent also noticed that her last admission came reluctantly, but knew better than to comment on it. "Jet lag can be the very devil—I can testify to that."

"Where do you start from—on your trips across the Atlantic?"

"Texas. How about you?"

"California. It took even longer this time because I changed planes in New York." She shook her head, remembering. "I thought I'd never get here."

"Only to be met on the doorstep by a fellow tenant. I'm sorry," he said ruefully. "I didn't mean to upset you even more."

Her lips twitched. "I was such a nervous wreck that I fell sound asleep in my clothes. Lord knows how many hours ago it was." It suddenly dawned on her that she still hadn't combed her hair or changed and color rose in her cheeks under his amused gaze. "I shouldn't keep rambling on . . ."

"My fault," Kent said, brushing it aside as he turned toward the bathroom. "I'll move my stuff in the medicine cabinet—it won't take a minute."

"Fair enough." She made her tone businesslike, hoping it sounded as if she'd spent several of her twenty-four years telling strange men to make themselves at home. "I'll just go in the dressing room in the meantime," she added, and then glanced over her shoulder to find that he'd already disappeared in the bathroom and closed the door. "Oh, Lord," she muttered and put up her palms to cool her hot face.

It took the utter chaos of scattered belongings on the floor of the dressing room to bring her back to normal. A surge of unreasoning anger rose in her and she stormed back to beat on the bathroom door.

"Hey, you don't have to get violent," Kent said with amusement, opening it a second later. "I'm just about finished . . ." his voice trailed off as he saw her furious expression. "What in the devil's the matter?"

"That's what I should be asking you. If this is your idea of a joke, I don't see the humor of it." She gestured wildly toward the other room. "Just clean up that clutter in there and leave. As fast as possible."

"What do you mean clutter?" he asked, scowling down at her. "What are you talking about?"

"As if you didn't know." She made no attempt to hide her scorn. "Just get it out of here."

He stared at her with narrowed eyes for an instant and then strode past her into the living room.

As he stood there, looking around, she came up behind him and pointed dramatically toward the dressing room. "Don't try to play the innocent with me."

"And you can stop acting like Poor Pitiful Pearl in a melodrama," he said, giving her an annoyed glance as he started toward the dressing room. "Anybody would think—bloody hell! What have you been doing?" The last came out forcefully as he saw his open bag and his belongings scattered ruthlessly around the floor.

Barbara was so angry that it took a moment to get her voice under control. "Oh, that's great! You actually think that *I* did that?"

"Well, I know damned well that I didn't." He gave her a hard stare. "Maybe you walk in your sleep."

"And maybe you escaped from Bedlam yesterday and came back in the middle of the night to pay me out."

"By lousing up my own belongings?" He shot a disgusted look her way. "You can do better than that."

The color rose in her cheeks again. "Well, then—what *did* happen?"

He rubbed the back of his neck and shook his head. "Damned if I know. There is one thing we can do, though."

"What's that?"

"Call Janice and find out if there are any other keys to this flat floating around." Suiting his action to the words, he went back to the living room and pushed the blankets back on her makeshift bed so that he could sit down by the telephone. Barbara noticed that there wasn't any hesitation as he dialed the rental agent's number. Obviously they were more than mere acquaintances—unless he possessed a photographic memory along with his other assets.

Her glance lingered on his smooth-shaven face until she remembered that she still hadn't done anything about improving her own appearance. She was torn between disappearing discreetly into the bathroom and an overriding curiosity to hear what Janice Carling would report.

Noticing that his mouth was settling into a grim line, she gathered they weren't going to get any answers just then. He hung up and turned to her to confirm it. "Jan isn't home and her answering machine isn't turned on so there's no telling when she'll be back. I thought you were going to get ready."

"I was. I mean, I am. What are you going to do?"

"Sit here and try to figure out what happened if you'll give me a chance."

Indignation made her mouth drop open. "Well, I like that," she managed to say finally.

"This isn't the time for you to get all hot and bothered," he pointed out, "and I doubt if you have the strength for it. If you don't get moving, there won't be anything decent left at the coffee bar."

"I can't believe it. There's a classic case of breaking and entering right next door," she said, gesturing toward the dressing room, "and all you can think about is a Danish pastry to go with your coffee."

"Well, it's a little late now to chew the scenery. Besides, that lock wasn't broken on the front door so there's no use even reporting it until we find out from Janice if there are any extra keys."

"I don't care how many keys there are—this is *my* flat for the time being. Your Mrs. Carling took my rent check—" She stopped abruptly as she saw Kent's mouth curve in amusement. "I suppose you're going to say that she took your check, too."

"Maybe we should give her the benefit of doubt until she can explain."

"Frankly, I think she's pretty absentminded to make a double booking," Barbara said with some acerbity. "A triple booking would mean that she's a confirmed idiot or she's a full-fledged swindler on the side."

"You'd better not go around making accusations like that or you'll be hauled into court."

"*I'll* be hauled into court?" Barbara's voice rose in disbelief. "I'm not the one who did the breaking and entering."

"Calm down. I'm just advising you to find out the whole story."

"Well, it's nice to know whose side you're on." Barbara drew herself up to her full five foot four. "I've decided I'm not hungry, so you go ahead." She went out to the front hall and opened the door, waiting for him to follow before saying sweetly, "I'll remember to put the chain on after you leave."

Kent gave her a flinty-eyed glance and then shook his head. "Okay, so I was out of line," he said finally, reaching over to close the door again. "I apologize. Now—will you please come for coffee with me?"

She stared at him in some confusion. If her rapid assessment were right, he looked as if he really meant the invitation. "All right," she said, deciding to follow her instincts. "It won't take me long."

His smile made him seem much more approachable. "Right. I'll clean up the dressing room and then make a couple more phone calls while I'm waiting—if you don't mind." The last phrase was tacked on diplomatically.

"Of course not—but I'm wondering if we should move anything in the dressing room. Don't we have to report this to the police?"

"You'd need to hang around so they could survey the place and make reports," Kent said carefully. "And from what I've heard about the flat's owner, he won't welcome any publicity."

"You know who the owner is?" she asked in surprise.

"I understand he's in some government ministry," Kent replied.

"I see." Barbara had followed him to the dressing room and stared around her with distaste. "You're right—it would be awful to have to live with this very long."

"And I doubt if even Sherlock Holmes could make much out of my wrinkled shirts," Kent said, picking one up from the corner. "At least there aren't any holes in it."

"It was probably just somebody hoping for a stereo or the family silver—anything that could be easily turned into money," Barbara said and reached for her robe. "If he'd gone through my suitcase, the haul would have been even leaner." She lingered by the door on her way out. "Have you found anything missing?"

"I don't think so." Kent's voice was muffled as he bent over his suitcase on the floor. "I'll check it out, though."

"Okay." She felt happier to have put all the decision making behind her and headed for the bathroom, saying lightly over her shoulder, "I'll expect a complete crime report when I come out."

Fortunately there was plenty of hot water and, although the rest of the flat's furnishings were miniscule, the tub and shower were of normal size. Once Barbara toweled herself dry, she slipped into her short nylon travel robe and un-zipped her cosmetic bag. Five minutes more and her reflection in the mirror revealed a considerable transformation. She was just applying a final touch of cherry lipstick to go with the linen coatdress of the same shade which she planned to wear, when she heard a penetrating buzz.

She opened the bathroom door to stick her head outside—almost colliding with Kent who was en route to a phone hanging on the wall by the front door.

"Hullo," he said guardedly into the mouthpiece and then, after an instant, his expression relaxed, "Hi! I've been trying to get in touch with you." The response must have been amusing because his grin appeared and he said, "Do tell. Well, we'll be expecting you." Hanging up the receiver, he pushed a button on the wall close by. "Building security," he reported unnecessarily as he turned to face Barbara who was half-hidden behind the bathroom door. "That was Jan—Mrs. Car-ling."

"So I gathered," she said dryly.

"She's on her way up."

"I figured that out, too."

Her cool response made his eyebrows go up, but that was all. "I didn't think you were in any condition to answer the phone," he said, finally opening the flat door as the elevator could be heard arriving. "I'll go and do the honors for you," he added, showing that he hadn't missed her near-transparent attire.

He pulled the apartment door almost closed behind him as he went out to greet the rental agent. With more enthusiasm than was called for, Barbara decided, taking the opportunity to make a dash for the dressing room in her lightly-clad state. She'd only taken two steps before a breathless, "Kent, darling," floated in from the hallway. Barbara risked a slight detour and peered around the edge of the front door.

An instant later, she found that she needn't have worried about being seen because Kent Michaels and a diminutive brunette were enveloped in a bear hug. But even her brief glance at the woman showed why Janice Carling's clients met her with open arms. She had a trim, perfectly proportioned figure revealed by a royal-blue raincoat with designer touches in every line. Her black hair was short and styled sleekly to her head and, from what Barbara could see of her features, they had the classic lines of a Raphael painting. It would have been easier to judge them if she hadn't been burrowing into Kent's broad shoulder at the moment with every evidence of enjoyment.

Barbara watched for a moment longer, and then drew back into the apartment hallway. There was no need for her to hurry into the dressing room; from the looks of that embrace, she'd have plenty of time to get dressed and repack her suitcase. After that she could phone around for a hotel reservation, because there was no doubt who'd be the eventual occupant of the flat if Janice Carling cast the deciding vote.

As Londoners would say—it was no contest at all.

❦ 2 ❧

Barbara's forebodings were confirmed by the fact that she was buttoning her coat-dress by the time she heard the front door hit the wall as Kent pushed it all the way open. "Barbara?" he called out, staying diplomatically in the foyer.

"I'm in here," she said, poking her head around the doorjamb of the dressing room. "Where's Mrs. Carling?"

"Holding the elevator for me." He went on quickly before she could comment. "I told her you'd just gotten up and she agreed that we'd better hold our conference over coffee. We'll save a place for you so you won't have to hurry."

"I don't know where this restaurant is," she protested. "Maybe I'd better skip the whole thing."

His calm demeanor changed back to the more familiar frown. "Don't be ridiculous," he snapped. "Just go up to Jermyn Street and turn right. The coffee bar's on the left-hand side—it's not more than three or four minute's walk and you can't miss it."

"Well, I suppose—"

"Fine," he cut into her words incisively. "We'll see you there."

Barbara found herself staring at the closed front door. "Damn!" she said, wishing she could have been more explicit and said it again when she heard Mrs. Carling's trill of laughter and the closing of the elevator door.

It would serve them both right if she ignored their invitation—no, make that an order—and got her own breakfast in the flat. She considered it as she adjusted the matching cherry leather belt around her waist and slipped into a pair of comfortable pumps. The disadvantage to such a tactic was that then she wouldn't even have a prayer of keeping the flat. Mrs. Carling would send back her check along with a polite request to vacate the premises as soon as possible. Which meant that she'd better get down to that coffee bar and at least make a stab at protecting her interests, Barbara decided.

She reached for her lavender travel raincoat and shrugged into it, knowing that she wasn't any competition for the rental agent in the fashion stakes. On the other hand, she looked a lot better than she had when Kent Michaels had first arrived on the scene.

Making sure that the apartment door was securely locked behind her, she went down the tiny elevator and again made sure that the outer door closed before going out onto the street. The sun was still trying to become a force, but it was the underdog when compared to the dark clouds encroaching from the north. It was easy to see that Londoners didn't have much faith in the outcome, because they were wearing raincoats or carrying rolled-up umbrellas. Barbara took a satisfying breath of the fresh morning air and turned up toward Jermyn Street a half block away. There were even more smart European clothes shops than she'd remembered and she decided that it was a good thing the exorbitant price tags in the display windows didn't encourage loitering. She cut across the narrow one-way street, checking the traffic first so that she wouldn't become another American pedestrian casualty—one of hundreds who look the wrong way at British intersections.

An attractive coffee bar was advertised farther down the block and she wasn't surprised to see Kent Michaels and the elusive Mrs. Carling at a round table by the window.

Evidently Kent was the only one who was keeping a watching brief, because he immediately beckoned to her and started getting to his feet. Mrs. Carling tore her attention from his face with evident reluctance and the smile she pinned on her face was just a little tardy.

She managed, however, to get in the first word when Barbara approached their table. "Miss Stratton," she said in a lilting voice whose undertones resembled the syrup that reposed in a jar on the table. "I'm so pleased to meet you at last. Kent has told me such nice things about you. Do sit down."

She gestured toward the empty chair at her side, ignoring the chair which Kent had pulled out next to him. Barbara wavered, uncertain what to do, until Kent took her arm and propelled her into the chair which he was holding.

"Thank you," Barbara told him in a tone that barely concealed her annoyance at his high-handed gesture. She rubbed her elbow where her skin still tingled. "I hope I didn't keep you waiting," she said, directing her attention to the rental agent.

"Hardly." Janice Carling pointed toward the cups of coffee in front of them. "I really didn't need this, but Kent said that you still haven't had any breakfast. Probably you'd prefer something more substantial," she added as a waitress approached.

"No, thank you," Barbara said, ignoring the implication that she consumed four-egg omelets and a stack of hotcakes to start the day. "Did you say something about a sweet roll?" she asked Kent when he gestured to the waitress that an-other cup of coffee was needed at the table.

He nodded. "The British version of cinnamon buns today. That's what I'm having. You'd better join me. Jan's on a diet," he added, looking amused.

"I never diet," the brunette retorted, her calm ruffled for the first time. "If one eats sensibly, dieting isn't necessary. It's simply a matter of self-discipline."

"Mmmm." Kent didn't sound convinced and looked on approvingly as the two mammoth cinnamon rolls stuffed with currants were deposited at their table together with a generous serving of butter. "Self-discipline may work for you, but Barbara and I need to keep our strength up—considering what's in front of us."

"I don't understand . . . ," Barbara began, a premonition of dread stealing over her. "Are you talking about the flat or the break-in?"

"Both, my dear." Janice put out a shapely hand in a sympathetic gesture toward Kent and then withdrew it hurriedly when she encountered a barrier of crockery and pastry. "I can't tell you how badly I feel about double booking you. It's never happened before, but I suppose there's always a first time."

The woman's soulful expression was masterful and, at any other time, Barbara would have been more impressed. Unfortunately, her first sip of coffee tasted warmed-over and bitter—which matched her own feeling at hearing that she probably no longer had a roof over her head. Even Janice Carling's charming British accent didn't improve the facts. To Barbara's way of thinking, the accent was just a little too perfect and made her suspect that the rental agent's manners might not be more than skin deep—no matter how elegant that outer layer.

"Jan, I thought we were going to talk about

this later on," Kent said, sounding businesslike and firm. "There's no point in spoiling Barbara's breakfast."

"I'd just as soon find out so I can try to make other plans," Barbara informed him, reaching to take another sip of coffee and then pushing the cup away. "Although that's not going to be easy. Reservations in London can be difficult any time."

"And this week more than ever, I'm afraid," Janice Carling said. She chewed delicately on her lower lip as she thought about it. "There's an international bar convention taking up all the available hotel space from what I've read. That's why I feel so badly about making this mistake in letting that flat. And then to have a break-in, besides." She shook her sleek head. "There's never been anything like it in that building to my knowledge. It's absolutely shocking."

Her dialogue sounded like an excerpt from *My Fair Lady*, Barbara thought as she replied, "It really wasn't so bad—considering that I slept through it."

"And they weren't your belongings," Kent added. "You don't happen to have a spare iron with you, do you?"

"Darling—you should have mentioned it before," Janice cut in before Barbara could answer. "I can take care of everything for you. There's a wonderful laundry in my neighborhood. Just bring your things around."

"Thanks, I'll remember," he said noncommittally.

Barbara took another bite of her cinnamon roll and then decided she wasn't very hungry, after all. It was all very well to sit and discuss Kent Michaels' wrinkled shirts, but she should be back at the flat and using the phone to try and find a place to stay. She tried to keep her voice casual as she told the other two, "If you'll excuse me— I'd better start beating the bushes for a roof. I presume that you can give me a refund on my rent money?" she asked Janice.

"Well, I suppose so—" the brunette started to reply, only to be cut off by Kent.

"There's no need for anything so drastic. I think there's a simpler solution if we all relax and keep our heads."

"But you said the flat was double booked," Barbara said, thoroughly confused as she stared at him. "Obviously you were there first." Her expression turned hopeful. "Unless you've decided that you'd rather be somewhere else—considering the break-in and everything."

He looked amused. "You're supposed to be a frail female who calls it quits—not the other way around."

"That isn't the reason I was giving up . . ."

"Well, there's no point in going on about it," Janice said, putting her napkin on the table and getting to her feet as if she didn't have any more time to waste. She spared a thin smile for Barbara before saying, "You'd best let Kent explain it. He's better at these things."

"But I'll have to have a refund on my deposit

if I'm going to look around . . ." Barbara said, knowing that her traveler's checks couldn't cope with too many emergencies.

"Don't worry about the financial side. It'll be all right—I promise you," Kent said in a firm tone as he got to his feet in deference to Janice's leaving.

The brunette's smile stayed in place but it was obviously an effort to keep it there. "About that wrinkled laundry of yours," she said provocatively to Kent, her head tilted like a sleek, glossy bird. "Are you going to take up my offer?"

"I might just do that. Let's wait and see. I'll be in touch."

Color flooded her cheekbones, showing she didn't often receive such a tempered response to her offers. Since most of the men in the coffee bar were giving her admiring glances, Barbara noted, it wasn't surprising.

Janice knew better than to belabor the point. "All right, darling. We'll leave it that way." She nodded and pulled the belt on her raincoat tighter as she walked to the door.

Barbara wasn't astonished to see a taxi pull up as soon as the rental agent gestured from the curb. As it drove off, she turned to Kent who had been watching the scene, too, with an enigmatic expression on his face.

"More coffee?" he said calmly, sitting down again.

"Oh, no!" The words were out before Barbara realized how impolite they sounded. "I mean, no thank you—not right now." She sat up straighter. "Could we please get this flat occupancy settled? I want to know one way or another. Are we flipping a coin or what?"

"If we did—we'd both lose, I'm afraid."

"Because I simply have to . . ." Her voice trailed off as his words registered. "What do you mean?" she got out finally.

"Just that. There's some emergency maintenance due. The last windstorm damaged the roof and they're having to replace it. That means our flat will be untenable most of the week. Janice was just notified this morning."

Barbara stared at him and then shook her head slowly. "That's one thing I didn't expect. Honestly, this trip is taking on all the aspects of a five-star nightmare."

He nodded in sympathy. "And Jan couldn't even cooperate about returning our rent money. She'd forwarded it to the owner and now he's out of town. We'll get the refund, but it's apt to take a while."

"The checks take a little longer."

He frowned at that and said, "I don't follow you."

"You know that old saying about mail delivery—'the bills go right through, but the checks always take a little longer.' " She rested her chin on her hand as she tried to think. "Can't Mrs. Carling give us a refund right away?"

"Jan?" He looked amused. "I doubt if there's enough left in her checking account for fish and chips tonight."

"I'd never imagine it from her clothes."

"I know." Kent sounded sympathetic, but he didn't mince words. "We can't really blame her for this roof fiasco—that was beyond her control."

Barbara managed a crooked smile. "Let's hope there are some dandy bed and breakfast places available. You can bunk in with that friend of yours, can't you? The place you stayed last night?"

"Nope. I've been tossed out, too. He has relatives from Scotland arriving today." Kent took a last swallow of coffee and gestured for the check. "At least, we still have the flat tonight—if you don't mind sharing."

The prospect of another night at the flat with a cat burglar on the loose made Barbara reconsider the proprieties. Then, too, it was hard to object to sharing four walls when her only alternative was deficit financing. Although if anyone had told her on her arrival at Heathrow that she'd be sharing her flat with a virtual stranger, she would have suspected them of wearing a white coat with sleeves that belted in the back.

Kent must have surmised the way her thoughts were going because he said sympathetically, "I'm sorry about this, but there's no need to worry. After all, there's space for a bed in the dressing room so we won't have to get under each other's feet."

It was hard to argue against his logic and, as he paid the check, Barbara decided it was foolish to cause herself unnecessary trouble. After all, he could have been obnoxious over priorities at the flat earlier on and he hadn't. As a matter of fact, he'd been more than generous about everything, she decided as they made their way out to the sidewalk. The least she could do was mention it. "You're being awfully nice about this," she began.

"One cup of lukewarm coffee and a cinnamon roll." His eyebrows rose at her praise. "There's no need to feel beholden for that."

"That's not what I meant." She tried to start over. "Except I wanted to thank you for that, too. What I really was talking about was the flat. I'm surprised that you didn't throw me out yesterday—since you were there first."

"I couldn't do that. You were too tired to fight back—properly." His grin showed as he pulled her to a stop beside the curb. "Look—I have the beginnings of an idea that might solve things for both of us this week while we're dispossessed." As he saw her suddenly skeptical expression, he emphasized, "A legitimate idea. I thought you were beginning to trust me."

"I am." She looked around them at the busy sidewalk. "Maybe we could finish this somewhere else."

He nodded, moving her aside as a man with a pushcart came by. "You have a point there. Are you going back to the flat now?"

"I guess so."

"All right." Kent was all business again. "I'll meet you there in twenty minutes. There's something I have to take care of at the Brit Rail office, but it's just around the corner so I shouldn't be long. And don't make any plans for the next couple of hours until I talk to you. Okay?"

Barbara nodded dazedly, hardly hearing his satisfied murmur of "Good," before he turned and started back the way they'd come. A moment later she realized that she was gaping after him like some star-struck groupie and walked hurriedly on, grateful that he hadn't checked to see if she'd followed his orders.

There was a thin, beaky-nosed man peering at the call boxes of her building when she arrived. Barbara hesitated, unwilling to interrupt him to unlock the front door. Then he became aware of her hovering figure and stepped out of her way, saying, "I beg your pardon. Rather close quarters here."

"It seems to be," she replied, putting the heavy brass key into the hole and wondering again why the owners couldn't have found something that didn't weigh a ton and take up most of her handbag.

"Look here . . ."

The man came up beside her on the step and she gave him a surprised glance.

"You couldn't possibly be Miss Stratton, could you?"

"Why yes," she said slowly, "but how did you know?"

A sudden grin lightened his face and took away his professorial look. "Well, I knew this was the right address and that American accent of yours did the rest. I'm Derek Redmayne," he added, extending his hand. "And I'm awfully glad I caught you in. I had Aunt Margaret's letter that you were coming."

"I didn't want her to bother you," Barbara said, remembering her losing battle with a neighbor back home. "There's nothing worse than to have an unknown tourist foisted on you."

"That might have been my first reaction, but I've certainly changed my mind," he said gallantly.

She suddenly remembered that she had the door halfway open. "Won't you come up to the flat? Perhaps you'd like some tea or something?"

"What rotten luck!" He brushed back a lock of his thick dark hair that flopped over his forehead. "Wouldn't you know it would work out like this? You've caught me on the way to Victoria Station—I'm due in Brighton at my shop there. Unfortunately, I made the arrangements before I knew that you were coming. I'll be back next week," he added hastily before she could get a word in. "Let's plan on getting together for dinner then. You can come and inspect my Knightsbridge shop afterward if you'd like."

Barbara thought she would, because her neighbor had already reported on his success in the antique field and how he had two thriving shops to prove it. What she hadn't known was that he'd turn out to be in his thirties with such a pleasant, outgoing manner. While his dark hair was worn longer than the current fashion at home and his magenta-striped shirt with its white collar was more trendy than understated Savile Row, it was impossible to fault anything else. He looked like a rare bird in the midst of the gray landscape and she decided it was just the cheering note she needed. Especially after sharing a breakfast table with Janice Carling. "That sounds very nice," she told him. "I'll look forward to it."

"Good." He beamed down at her on the step. "After this I'll pay proper attention to my aunt's letters. Is there any chance you'll be coming to Brighton in the next day or so?"

Barbara almost confessed that she was going to have to spend her spare time hunting for lodgings rather than following the antique circuit, but was reluctant to bare her soul. Besides, there was always the chance that Kent might know of a solution—certainly he had hinted at the possibility. "I rather doubt it," she told Derek finally. "There's a long list of things I want to see and it's hard to fit everything in."

"I understand." He cast a quick glance at his watch and grimaced. "Well, I'd best be off. Take care and I'll be in touch as soon as I'm back in town." He'd taken a step toward the street before he snapped his fingers and turned back. "I *am* an idiot. Do you know, I don't have your phone number. My aunt just forwarded this address."

"I'm not sure myself," Barbara told him. "Rather than have you wait and maybe miss your train—I'll leave it at your shop here in London." Inwardly she was thinking that the dodge would cover any possible move she might make in the meantime.

"Right-e-oh." He managed to combine his hailing of a taxi with his gesture of farewell. "Until then."

Barbara stared at his retreating cab with a bemused expression. She'd heard British comics say "right-e-oh" on television, but it hadn't occurred to her that it was ever used in ordinary conversation.

She was still smiling about it as she waited for the elevator and it had just arrived when she heard the front door open again.

"Hold it," came Kent's voice, stopping her halfway into the lift.

He came striding through the hall and squeezed in the small space beside her. "Okay, let 'er rip."

"Right-e-oh." The expression came out before she thought and she felt his tall figure stiffen.

"What did you say?" Obviously he hadn't believed his ears.

"I said 'right,'" she told him briskly, hoping the grinding of the elevator motor would cover her flagrant lie. Not for anything would she try to explain her lapse. "Why do you ask?"

He opened his mouth as if tempted to argue and then shrugged as they arrived at their level. "It isn't important," he said as they got out and walked toward the flat. "I didn't know that I'd be so close on your heels."

"Well, actually—I met a friend." As long as she'd started telling whoppers, she might as well do it right, Barbara thought. It wouldn't hurt Kent to think that she was surrounded by admirers so that he wouldn't be tempted with his King Cophetua role. Damned if she'd play an obliging beggar-maid, no matter how accurate the casting!

He had his key out and was unlocking the door. "I thought I saw you on the doorstep as I came 'round the corner. You should have said that you planned to meet someone—I didn't mean to interfere with your social life."

"You didn't," she said coolly, sweeping by him into the flat's tiny foyer. "Derek was just on his way to catch a train."

"Going out of town, is he?"

She caught a tone of satisfaction in Kent's murmured response and enjoyed saying, "Only to Brighton. He has business interests down there."

If Kent were disconcerted by her reply, it wasn't apparent. He simply nodded and went to perch on the end of the divan where she'd spent the night.

"Speaking of business," he said, watching her put down her purse on the end table and shrug out of her raincoat, "I wonder if I could persuade you to help me out. The weather's halfway decent this morning and I need a model."

Barbara had been going to hang her coat in the big armoire-type closet in the dressing room, but she stopped on the threshold. "Model?" She shot him a puzzled glance. "I don't understand. What kind of work do you do?"

"I thought I'd told you." He stretched his long legs out in front of him, taking up a good portion of the tiny living room. "I'm a photographer—calendar shots mostly." Looking up to see her suddenly disapproving look, he started to chuckle. "You don't have to worry. I specialize in a different type of calendar—mostly buildings and landscape shots. While I'm here this time, I'm hoping for some Roman ruins—I've already photographed Stonehenge and a few cathedrals."

"That's all very well," Barbara said, still suspicious, "but the closest Roman ruin must be Bath and it would be the middle of the afternoon before we could get there."

"Ruins aren't the only things I have on my list. There's a pair of pandas at the Regent Park Zoo that are good calendar fare and they'll look even better with a pretty girl to frame the picture. Can you spare the time? We can work out a day rate for you later." He cast a quick glance through the window. "The weather's tricky over here. I'd like to be there before the sun disappears altogether."

"You know what they say about English weather—'if you don't like it, just wait twenty minutes and you'll have something new.' "

Kent responded with a slight smile, but he shook his head as he got up to rummage in his suitcase. "From the looks of the clouds on the horizon, I'd say that 'something new' in this case means a choice of rain or thunder. That's why I'm carrying a raincoat and I'd advise you to do the same."

"Hey, wait a minute. I haven't said that I'll go with you."

"Have you something better in mind?"

"Well, no—but that doesn't mean that you can just go around arranging my life."

"My dear girl, it's a good, easy way to make some extra money and if we're about to be tossed out of this flat . . ." He shrugged and let her figure out the consequences as he carefully extracted a soft leather pouch with a strap from his suitcase.

"What's that?"

"My camera." He reached for two boxes of film and stuffed them in his raincoat pocket. "It goes with the territory when you're taking pictures."

"You don't have to be sarcastic about it," she pointed out, not bothering to hide her annoyance either. "It was a perfectly civil question."

"All right. I apologize." He unzipped the case and offered it for her inspection. "One Hasselblad—as advertised. Now, do I have a model or don't I?"

"What will you do if I don't go with you?"

"Probably pick up a visitor on the scene. It isn't difficult, but I'd rather not bother with explanations and releases."

Barbara hesitated just a moment longer, well aware that he wouldn't have any trouble finding someone at the zoo to fill his requirements. Probably his only problem would be getting the model off his hands afterward. She watched as he shrugged into his beige raincoat and wound the strap of the camera case carefully around his hand. Then he looked inquiringly across the room at her.

"All right—I'm coming." She picked up her

own raincoat and made sure she had a waterproof square for her hair. "It's a pity that we can't get this lock changed," she said as they went out in the foyer.

"It might help your peace of mind, but if somebody wants in—they'll get in," he said laconically, closing the door behind them. "I wouldn't worry about it now—unless you've any crown jewels in your bags."

Barbara punched the button for the elevator with unnecessary force. "I left them at home this trip. Besides, they weren't interested in my stuff— obviously yours was of higher quality."

He let his glance run quickly over her. It was a thorough masculine appraisal without missing an inch on the way, and brought the color flooding to her face. "You underestimate yourself," he said matter-of-factly as the elevator ground to a halt and the door opened.

There was silence after that until they reached the main floor and were on their way to the street. Then she managed to ask, "How do we get to the zoo from here?"

He shot her a quizzical glance. "What would you like to do?"

"If there's time—could we take a bus?"

"I don't see why not." He made sure the entrance door to the apartment house locked before following her down the steps. "My expense account would even cover a taxi if you'd rather."

"A double-decker bus will be fine. That way I can rubberneck on the way. Where do we catch one?"

"Just a block away at Regent Street."

"Wonderful!" She looked back over her shoulder before they turned the corner at Jermyn Street. "The flat's in a marvelous location. It's going to be hard to find anything half so good at a rate I can afford."

"I know what you mean." Kent put a protective hand in front of his camera case as they made their way along the crowded sidewalk toward Regent Street. "Maybe something can be worked out. Let's take it a little at a time."

Which meant that he didn't want to talk about it anymore, Barbara thought, and she really couldn't blame him. She wasn't keen to dwell on being dispossessed right then either. It would be better to enjoy this unexpected trip to the zoo and the rare sunshine that was still bathing Mayfair in its gentle warmth.

Their trip out to Regent's Park was a delight. Near Piccadilly there were the wonderful shops on view as the bus lurched along in the bumper-to-bumper traffic. Displays of china and fine fabrics vied with other windows filled with leather and jewelry that would have delighted a maharaja. When the elegant retail shops finally thinned to neighborhood hotels and office buildings, Kent remembered to ask the bus conductor if he'd tell them when they reached the zoo stop. The man beamed and announced he'd be glad to. "Not long now, guv," he promised. "I'll let you know."

"He's certainly nice about it," Barbara murmured when the man went on down the aisle collecting fares.

Kent nodded. "Most of them are." He started to chuckle. "Not all of the residents agree on that though. There was a comment in the paper about it the other day. Someone wrote in to complain about the British Rail ticket sellers. Said that the BR stands for 'bloody rude.' This must be our stop—the conductor's beckoning."

It was only as they were getting off that the conductor mentioned the zoo entrance gate was almost a mile away. As they walked down the quiet sidewalk toward it, Barbara gave silent thanks that she was wearing comfortable shoes. When she glanced up at Kent by her side, she discovered a preoccupied expression on his face. "Is something wrong?" she got up her courage to ask.

He hesitated visibly before saying, "What makes you think that?"

Probably because he was answering her question with another one, Barbara thought. Aloud she merely said, "You appeared to be miles away. Not that it's any of my affair."

He shook his head. "Sorry. Actually I was trying to think of a different shot for the pandas and wondering if they'll cooperate."

"And I thought you only had to worry about the weather—plus an amateur model."

His pace slowed momentarily as he gave her another of those raking appraisals. "Does that mean you haven't modeled before? With your measurements and the way you move—I would have thought you were a natural."

"I worked in our local department store shows during one college vacation," she admitted, "but that was four or five years ago."

His grin taunted her. "Should I tell you it's like riding a bicycle?"

"Not if you want to arrive at the zoo in one piece."

"Okay, I won't say it then." His eyes narrowed as he bestowed another sideways glance. "What do you do for a living these days?"

"If you keep up this attempt at a four-minute mile, I'll be a complete wreck when I get back home and not fit for anything," she said, abandoning the pretense that she could keep up with his long strides.

"Sorry." He slackened his pace instantly. "I'm getting absentminded since I've been over here."

"That's all right," she said, happy to see that austere expression of his disappear for the moment. "The only jogging I've done lately is down to the local ice cream parlor, so I'm out of condition." When his eyebrows rose skeptically, she added, "It's true—I'm just lucky it doesn't show on my waistline. Besides, I lose weight when I travel so I indulged a little before I left home."

"And where is home?"

"California. San Francisco originally." She thought for an instant about asking some questions herself, but decided there might be a better time. They were coming up behind a column of preschoolers being shepherded along the sidewalk by their teacher and two or three anxious mothers. Since their pace was slow, Kent caught her hand and they edged single file around the serpentine.

"That looks like the zoo gate down there in the middle of the block," Kent said, releasing her fingers once they had the sidewalk to themselves again.

"I'm glad. If those pandas are having brunch when we get there, I might ask to join the party," she told him, keeping her tone light. Inwardly she wasn't sure whether to be glad that he'd severed that casual contact once they were past the youngsters. There wasn't anything absentminded about his maneuver, she noted, and told herself she should be glad that he wasn't making any overtures when they'd barely scraped up an acquaintance.

"What's the matter?"

His concerned voice finally penetrated her thoughts and she glanced up, startled. "I beg your pardon?"

"You looked unhappy suddenly. I'm not going too fast for you, am I?"

"Anything but." The wry comment was out before she knew it. Quickly she added, "Everything's just fine. Oh, I'd forgotten that they charged an admission."

Fortunately, her babbling disconcerted him so he couldn't dwell on her indelicate outburst. "Don't worry about that. A model fits into my expense account quite legitimately. You should know that or"—he gave her a thoughtful look—

"don't you deal with expense accounts in your line of work?"

"I don't have very much to do with them," she said. When he let the silence lengthen, she went on, "I'm with a big design consulting firm, but on the lower rungs. In fact, I was terribly lucky to get the job in the first place because the competition was fierce."

"I see." Kent's tone didn't give away what he was thinking. "Did you meet Derek in your work?"

"Who?"

The moment she said it, Barbara could have knocked her head against the stone wall edging the sidewalk. To think she'd gone to all that trouble to provide a mystery man and then she had to get amnesia.

Kent's amused expression wasn't hard to translate either. "I meant your friend on the doorstep of the flat. Just before I came back."

"Oh, you mean *that* Derek," she said, trying to sound as if the name took up several pages in her address book. "He's sort of a—family acquaintance." She waved a hand airily. "You know how those things are."

It was a feeble response, but fortunately they turned in to the ticket seller's booth at the zoo entrance just then and the subject was dropped.

Once they went inside the gate, Barbara felt a surge of delight at visiting one of the most superb zoological parks in the world. The gardens alongside the swept cement walks were full of color and the buildings were carefully designed to fit in as a part of the landscape. A sudden padding noise behind her made her turn and then she started to laugh as she moved aside to let a young elephant and his keeper have the right of way. The youngster plodded by, not looking to left or right. The keeper by his head beamed down on him with pride, like a parent basking in the limelight of a favorite offspring.

Barbara heard the click of a shutter and turned to find Kent lowering his camera with a grin on his face. "Nothing good enough to publish," he told her, "but a nice memento just the same."

"He was a darling—much better than penguins for my money."

"What do penguins have to do with it?"

"John Ruskin wrote something about watching penguins in the zoo to get life in the right perspective. I'd head for the elephant house instead."

"Well, I'm afraid we'd better call on the pandas first," Kent said, casting a concerned look at the gathering clouds to the northwest. "Even now, the light's going to be a problem."

She nodded sympathetically. "Just tell me what you want me to do."

"The panda enclosure should be down the path over here," he said, gesturing to the left. "I'll go ahead and do some of the preliminaries. You can look around for a bit and meet me there in fifteen minutes or so."

It wasn't hard to fill her spare time, Barbara found. She started for the lion house, but found herself intrigued by a disdainful hippo, his skin still glistening from a bath. After giving her a disapproving look from the corner of his outdoor pen, he turned and trotted off, intent on finding something better to occupy his time.

"That for you, chum!" Barbara muttered and then felt absurd as an elderly couple edged away after hearing her talk to herself. She walked on, trying to look as purposeful as the hippo and found herself the only admirer at the outdoor enclosure housing a young gorilla. He, too, gave her a wary glance and pretended consuming interest in his rubber tire hanging close by. That didn't last and his wistful expression when he turned to see if she were still admiring him made Barbara murmur soft words of encouragement. They indulged in the mutual admiration society until she happened to glance at her watch and gasped to see how much time had passed.

"Take it easy," Kent said as she hurried around the corner of the big panda cage several minutes later, breathing hard. "You're not *that* late."

"I thought I was keeping an eye on my watch," she apologized. "At least the weather hasn't changed much."

"No, I'm afraid we're stuck with it. It would have been nice to have some white fleecy clouds for contrast," he said and then grinned as he saw her entranced expression. "I thought you'd seen these two before."

"No," she barely breathed the word, keeping her glance on the occupants of the enclosure who were giving their entire attention to the piles of bamboo in front of them. "And the pandas in Washington, D.C., were asleep when I visited there. Aren't we lucky to come at feeding time?"

"It wasn't entirely luck," Kent said dryly, adjusting his camera for the proper exposure. "They post the schedules for all the animals. Button up your coat and get over there by the corner of the cage. I'd like you in the left foreground—just a profile shot," he went on, checking his focus as she moved where he instructed. "The panda gets the starring role. I want to catch him when he's peeling a new stalk of bamboo."

Barbara grinned over her shoulder. "Discrimination if I ever heard it."

"Sue me," Kent said calmly. "A little bit more to your left. Now, lift your chin. That's it. Okay—just hang on. That damned bear would pick this time to go rooting around in the dirt."

"He's just trying to find a tasty morsel, I think," Barbara said, trying to keep her head at the angle Kent had approved and still see what was going on inside the cage.

"Never mind, you can relax. I'll have to wait now until that cloud passes and there's some decent sun." He shot an irritated look skyward. "Just when we have this place practically to ourselves, too."

Barbara nodded, relaxing as she glanced around the barrier. There was an Indian family group just leaving, the youngsters still talking excitedly about the pandas from their gestures. On the far side of the cage, an older man stood sketching, oblivious to everything except the two occupants. Another middle-aged man approaching along the path stopped to consult the direction sign post and then compared it with a brightly colored map of the zoo in his hand.

"Here we go." Kent's voice brought her out of her reverie as sun poured over the enclosure again when the cloud cover passed. "Tilt your head—no, the other way—that's it. Just stay like that."

Barbara obediently kept her gaze on the nearest panda which wasn't hard at all because he was sitting up, clutching a bamboo stalk and ripping off the outer layer of it with total accuracy. In the background, she heard the clicking of Kent's shutter, but with the tableau in front of her, it was easy to keep an entranced expression on her face. Before long, Kent said, "Okay—that should do it. I'll just—"

His words were interrupted by someone else saying, "I beg your pardon. Oh, I say—let me help you," and she turned to see the man who'd been checking his zoo map assisting Kent from a thick shrub. She hurried across the walk just as Kent managed to get upright at the edge of the path. The other man was red-faced with embarrassment, saying, "It was all my fault—I should have been watching where I was going instead of consulting this thing for directions."

"That's okay," Kent said, trying to brush some dry leaves from his coat sleeve with one hand while he still clutched the camera with the other. "I wasn't watching what I was doing either."

"Well, so long as there's no harm done." The stranger ducked his head in a nervous farewell which encompassed Barbara as well and almost scuttled down the path again.

"I think maybe he spoke too soon," she said, seeing the grimace of pain on Kent's face as he moved into the center of the path again. "Where does it—" she broke off as she realized that it wasn't diplomatic to ask a thirty-year-old man where it hurt. She managed to finish with a lame, "bother you?" which sounded as if she'd just enrolled in English for the Foreigner.

That must have occurred to Kent, too, because he frowned at her before saying tersely, "My ankle. I guess I twisted it when I stepped off the edge of the path. It'll be all right in a minute."

Privately Barbara doubted it when she saw how pale his face was after he managed to limp over to a nearby bench and sit down. "Do you want me to get some help?"

"What for?" It was obvious that the invalid role wasn't to his liking as his frown deepened. "It's not a broken leg, for God's sake."

"I just thought maybe someone should bandage it or look at it or something . . ."

"I'm looking at it and that's enough for now." His tone softened as he went on, "There's no need for this to spoil your visit to the zoo. Why don't you wander around and I'll wait here for you."

"No way," she said, her tone just as firm as his. "The animals can wait until another day. At least let me play Florence Nightingale, if you won't let me do anything else."

"It really isn't necessary . . ." he began and then his expression softened as he saw her face. "All right, we might as well scratch the rest of the visit. At least I think I got two decent pictures before falling into the shrubbery."

"So it isn't a total loss." She watched as he rose to his feet and tried putting some weight on his injured ankle. "Can you make it as far as the gate?"

He nodded, albeit grimly. "If you don't mind a heavy hand on your shoulder. Let's give it a try."

They started off at a measured pace and almost immediately Kent's arm came across her shoulder as he attempted to keep as much weight as possible from the sprain. "You're going to be about three inches shorter by the time we get to the gate," he told Barbara. As a group of teen-agers stared at them with unhidden interest, he added, "They probably think I've had a few too many."

"At this time of day?"

He didn't miss her scandalized tone. "It's been known to happen."

"But surely not when you're keeping company with the rhinos and sea lions. The locale's all wrong."

"I'll remember that if I'm tempted," he assured

her. "Hallelujah! I think we're finally getting to the promised land."

Barbara was equally happy to see the buildings surrounding the ticket booth looming ahead of them. Somewhere, she decided, there must be a public telephone so that she could call a taxi in case there wasn't one cruising outside the gate. Aloud, she said, "Why don't you sit on that low rock wall by the gift shop and I'll go out and try to flag a cab."

"There's no need for you to do all the work—"

"Look here," she said, interrupting him ruthlessly, "I wish you'd stop trying to act the macho male and use your head instead. If you stand on that ankle much longer, you'll be sorry later—especially when you have to go flat-hunting tomorrow."

"So I'm supposed to sit down and let you—"

". . . take over," she said, cutting him off again. "That's right." Urging him toward the wall, she waited until he'd settled gingerly atop it and then asked, "Shall I try for a cruising cab first?"

Kent was all set with a biting comment, but relented when he saw her pale, concerned face. "Okay. See what luck you have. If it were a little later, there'd be lots around. Anyhow, there's no hurry." His slow smile appeared. "This is a very comfortable rock."

"Even so, you should be getting some ice on your ankle."

He waved her toward the gate. "Stop fussing.

I'll sit quietly and indulge in omphaloskepsis."

"If you start contemplating your navel here, they'll be calling a keeper for you. Really, I don't know why I don't just leave you by yourself," she said, trying to keep her voice stern.

"Because Florence Nightingale would be sadly disappointed at such behavior," he informed her. "You'd better get on with it—we're attracting more attention than those two peacocks over there and the authorities won't approve."

Barbara stood on the curb beside the busy street rimming the zoo for the next five minutes or so, searching the oncoming traffic for a vacant taxi. Finally, when she'd decided that they were as extinct as the dodo bird, one pulled up at the gate to discharge an elderly couple. Two minutes later, she was helping Kent into it, settling beside him with a sigh of relief. She wasn't surprised to hear him give the address of the flat to the driver and waited until they'd started off before she said ruefully, "I don't suppose you'll consider seeing a doctor."

"Not unless it's worse in the morning. Under the circumstances, I hope we can reach an agreement for tonight."

Barbara's glance slid toward the driver beyond the half-open window partition. Since she had no intention of providing any soap opera-type dialogue, she replied, "There shouldn't be any problem—considering the circumstances *and* your ankle."

Kent's mouth quirked in amusement. "I didn't

think you'd miss that. Maybe you should be thankful."

"Next you'll have me believing that it was deliberate."

"Hardly. I had a lot of things I wanted to accomplish in the next few days so this is going to cause some monumental rescheduling. In the meantime, I wonder if I could interest you in a short cruise?"

Barbara forgot all about the taxi driver. "I thought I'd convinced you that propositions leave me cold. And you needn't try to use that 'helpless invalid' bit."

"I didn't intend to. I can't manage on a ship with this ankle so you'd be using my ticket." He shifted to get more comfortable after they'd turned a corner. "Why are you giving me such a funny look?"

"You don't happen to print money in your spare time, do you?"

"Not as a general rule." As he pushed back against the corner of the taxi seat to survey her more carefully, he asked, "Are you always so suspicious?"

"It's never happened before. There haven't been any of my acquaintances that gave cruise tickets away."

"This isn't a big deal either. Sort of a mini-cruise to Norway and back by way of the Shetland Islands. You could board at Southampton tomorrow." As he moved forward to emphasize his point, he must have twisted his ankle because he grimaced in pain. "Dammit-all! What a blasted nuisance!"

Barbara's visions of a gorgeous cruise ship vanished in an abrupt return to reality. "You're not going to feel like struggling out for dinner tonight. Actually, you should elevate your foot and put something cold on it for the rest of the day. Do you have an ice bag at the flat?"

Kent's brow wrinkled as he tried to remember. "An ice bucket but that's all." He looked at her hopefully. "Would you mind shopping for one?"

"Of course not." She glanced out the cab window and found that they were traveling along the edge of Hyde Park. "It would save time if I got out at the next traffic light and took another cab to Knightsbridge. I'll shop for an ice bag and, at the same time, buy something for dinner in the food halls at Harrods. Can you manage to get up to the flat on your own?" she asked, suddenly doubtful.

"If I take my time, there'll be no problem," he assured her and leaned forward to instruct the taxi driver. Then, before she knew what he was doing, he had extracted some pound notes from his wallet and tucked them inside her purse.

"Hey, what's that for?"

"Food and all the rest," he told her as the driver started to pull over to the curb.

"But I have money—"

"Good," he said, cutting her off briskly. "Then you might want to add to your wardrobe. They still dress for dinner on cruise ships and it's best to be prepared."

"But I haven't said I was going," she protested as the cab braked at the corner.

"No, but I'm hoping you will over dinner. Don't stop to argue now—we're blocking traffic," Kent said, leaning forward to open the door for her on the curb side. "There's a free cab right behind us if you get a move on. And if you have any extra spare change when you've finished your shopping . . ."

She stopped on the sidewalk to peer through the open taxi window at him. "Yes?"

"You might buy one of those *Norwegian for the Traveler* books for when you're aboard ship, and start your homework tonight." His grin was wicked. "After all, even Florence Nightingale must have had something to take her mind off her work."

3

It was barely an hour later before Barbara let herself into the flat again. She managed it with some difficulty because she was trying to keep two plastic shopping bags upright on the floor at her feet and hang onto a box of pastry with her free hand.

Kent must have heard her fumbling the key in the lock because his head poked around the doorjamb from the living room as she started shifting the plastic bags from the hallway into the flat. "I can help you with those," he began until Barbara froze him with an annoyed look.

"You're supposed to be lying down with your foot up—" She broke off to stare at his ankle suspiciously. "Unless you've made a miraculous recovery in the last hour."

"Hardly. It hurts like hell. I just thought it

sounded as if you were having trouble," he said, lingering in the doorway to watch her transferring the plastic bags onto the kitchen counter. "You must have enough in there for a banquet."

"The only similarity is the main course," she told him dryly. "We're having chicken and it comes frozen in little boxes just like home. If you'd rather, I could phone one of the restaurants in this block and see if I can get anything to take out—"

"Take-away," he cut in and when she looked mystified, he added, "Over here, it's take-away instead of take-out. You don't have to worry though—I'm an expert on chicken in little boxes. Is there anything to go with it?"

"If you don't get on the couch with your foot up, I'll change the entire menu to smoked mackerel with sliced apple on a bunch of watercress— that's what they're serving at the coffeehouse across the street plus slab cake for dessert."

"You're getting your strength back," Kent said, retreating to the couch under her threat. "It was better when you were suffering from jet lag."

"I can be much worse than this." She wrenched at the ice cube tray in the tiny refrigerator and finally extracted it with some effort. "You'd better take your shoe and sock off—I found an ice bag when I was shopping."

"The shoe's already off—it has been ever since I got back here. I'm surprised that you didn't notice."

The amusement in his voice showed that he wasn't surprised at all. He must have observed that she had merely cast a nervous glance his way when she came in, barely noting that he'd changed into a pair of cotton slacks and an open-throated tattersall sports shirt. It was obviously "something comfortable" and she found herself reluctant to dwell on that subject. Instead, she concentrated on getting the ice cubes into the narrow top of the rubberized bag without spilling them.

When she went into the living room a few minutes later carrying the ice bag and a towel, she found Kent lounging on the couch as he sorted through a handful of what appeared to be brightly colored brochures. "Do you want to put this on?" she asked, trying to sound brisk as she held the bag out to him.

"That was the general idea." His eyes narrowed as he stared up at her hovering figure. "Unless you have a better angle."

"Don't be ridiculous." She frowned as she saw him deposit it carelessly on his right foot. "Your ankle doesn't look very swollen."

"It feels like hell. What's the towel for?"

"In case the ice bag leaks. That pale-yellow couch cover won't improve with a soaking."

"Okay. Shove it under," he said, lifting his foot with a grimace. "After that, sit down and listen. You still have some more errands to run this afternoon and first off is a trip to the steamship office."

She stared at him solemnly. "Then you meant it—*really* meant it."

"About the cruise? Of course I did. I never joke about important things. Besides, I'm not being completely altruistic." He paused just long enough to move his foot into a more comfortable position. "I can use you for a model when I join you in Bergen after a day or so."

Barbara took the handful of brochures that he held out to her and looked through them, still unable to believe what was going on. "But if you come to Bergen, won't you need the ticket for the rest of the trip?"

"Probably just another plane ticket back to London. If there's any kind of weather in the North Sea, I don't want to be limping around on a slippery deck."

"It still doesn't seem fair." Barbara let her glance rest on the steamship ticket and drew a deep breath. The price listed at the bottom was more than she'd allotted for her whole trip to Britain and yet Kent was giving it up with scarcely a murmur. If she hadn't known better, she would have suspected that he'd fallen on his head rather than his ankle at the zoo.

He moved again on the couch, this time trying to shove a coral pillow behind his back to get comfortable. "I really must be losing my touch," he muttered. "I didn't think you'd have any objections to leaving London—since you can't stay here."

"I'm just now letting myself believe it," she

confessed and then raised a worried face to his. "But what about you? Where will you stay in the meantime?"

He shrugged. "It's Jan's turn to accept some responsibility. I may let her find an empty bed for me. For tonight, I can doss down in the dressing room or in here—whichever you'd prefer."

"We can work that out later." Even the most casual mention of Janice Carling made her stomach muscles tie themselves into knots. Which was ridiculous, Barbara told herself, and merely showed that she should have stopped for lunch somewhere along the way because breakfast had been practically nonexistent.

"Is this a habit of yours?"

Kent's wry comment finally penetrated and she asked absently, "What habit?"

"Going off into a brown study. I thought you'd be over the worst of jet lag by this time."

"I'm just hungry." She stood up and started toward the kitchen. "Shall I fix you a sandwich?"

"Not now." He sounded as if he were hanging onto his good humor with some effort. "I just *told* you—you have to get down to the steamship company and switch that ticket." Another thought evidently struck him because he frowned to ask, "You do have your passport with you, don't you?"

"Of course." She carefully tucked the papers he'd given her into her purse and reached for her coat again. "If somebody reports an emaciated and unidentified body in this neighborhood . . ."

"I'll let your parents know and tell them you were on an errand of mercy at the time," he assured her, getting up to follow her into the hall.

"You're supposed to be resting your foot," she said, giving him an exasperated look.

"I'll do that after I make myself a cup of coffee. That mention of a sandwich reminded me that it's past lunchtime." Her brooding expression made him add, "You'd better stop for something after you change the ticket."

"How thoughtful of you to mention it," she said in a tone that meant nothing of the kind and yanked open the hall door. "Don't expect me back by tea—I might go shopping."

"Good idea. Most women like to wear something special for the Captain's Dinner," he advised as he came over to hold the door.

The sound of another door opening down the hall made him stiffen and then, before Barbara realized what was happening, he'd yanked her into a close embrace. His mouth came down to cover hers in a brusque, hard kiss that had Barbara hanging onto his shoulders as her mind whirled into limbo.

She was only vaguely aware of a smothered whistle behind them and then footsteps clattering down the stairway beyond the elevator. As they faded from hearing, Kent pushed back and cocked his head, plainly listening.

Barbara swayed and put out her hand, groping for the wall as she tried to rejoin the world. "I don't know what . . . ," she began and saw that she wasn't getting his attention so she started again. "You had absolutely no right to do anything like—"

"Be quiet!" His terse command cut into her complaint and left her open-mouthed, staring at him in amazement.

She would have complained vigorously if she hadn't been stopped by his grim, listening expression. They stood like statues in the empty hallway until he evidently decided that there were to be no more visitors. "I'm sorry about that," Kent said then in a level, matter-of-fact tone. "Nosy neighbors annoy me and kissing you was the best way I could think of to spoil his view. You're okay, aren't you?"

It must have just dawned on him that she was having trouble getting her breathing under control and that her flushed face made her look like a refugee from a fever ward. She endured his kindly regard for another twenty seconds, while she tried to think of something sufficiently cutting to say and finally had to settle for, "I'm perfectly fine, thank you." Her chin went up defiantly. "Next time, don't involve me in your harebrained schemes."

"I wouldn't think of it," he assured her. "Get going now and be careful when you cross the street. You want to be in good shape for the trip."

Such a casual send-off did little to endear him to her and Barbara was still fuming when she let herself out the front door of the building a few minutes later. As she marched up to Jermyn Street to hail a cab, she decided that it was ridiculous to place any importance on one kiss. Certainly Kent Michaels wasn't letting it clutter up his mind. Barbara drew in a painful breath as she thought about it and then went on to the reluctant conclusion that if he could accomplish so much in an offhand gesture at the door, he could really curl a woman's toes on a davenport in the living room.

That fantasy was real enough that she shook her head and muttered, "Don't be disgusting." Unfortunately, she happened to be standing on the curb at the time alongside a middle-aged man who was vying for the same taxi. Her remark made him draw back, blinking in astonishment— while she got in the cab and was driven off.

By the time she'd exchanged the steamship ticket and finished a very satisfactory sandwich with two cups of tea, her mood had improved beyond recognition. Seeing a picture of her cabin on the ship and perusing the itinerary showing tempting ports of call did wonders for her morale.

So did the long royal-blue velveteen skirt that she purchased in Regent Street a little later, after deciding it would be versatile enough for dinner aboard ship when teamed with a chiffon blouse that she'd brought along.

By the time she'd stopped for another cup of tea and biscuits, she decided there was no use stalling any longer. It was ridiculous to be skulking around—literally walking the streets—when she was a bona fide, rent-paying tenant. She decided to splurge on another taxi since her feet felt as if they'd been worn down to her ankles by then. It was in the middle of the rush hour and she had to wait a considerable time before an empty cab came along. As they wended their way down the crowded streets toward Mayfair, she was looking guiltily at her watch.

When Barbara arrived at Duke of York Street and was going up in the tiny elevator, she had a vision of all the catastrophes that could have happened to Kent while she'd been away.

The sound of the BBC on the television as she unlocked the door of the flat showed that if Kent were suffering, it wasn't in the way she'd imagined. His casual call of, "Hi, is that you?" as she went in confirmed her suspicion.

"That depends who you're expecting," she said, wondering why she'd wasted a minute worrying about the man. She walked into the living room and saw him comfortably stretched out on the davenport with a drink at his elbow. "What happened to the towel?" she asked, raking him with a disapproving glance.

"The what?"

"Towel. T-O-W-E-L. The one you're supposed to have under your foot."

"Oh, that." He dismissed it with a shrug. "The ice bag doesn't leak. Did you get a dress?"

His question diverted her momentarily. "I don't see why that matters to you since you're not going on the cruise."

"It isn't number one on my list of priorities," he said, fixing her with an equally cool look, "but I gathered that box under your arm has something to do with your wardrobe. Most women would be dragging it out by now."

"I'm not most women. Besides, it's not a dress. Just a skirt." She quickly went in the dressing room to put it on her suitcase, and lingered there for a moment—not knowing whether to be relieved or annoyed because he'd obviously forgotten their embrace in the hallway earlier. So much for lasting impressions!

"Everything go all right at the steamship office?" he called from the living room.

"Yes, thanks." She put her coat in the closet and came back into the living room so that she could talk without raising her voice. "They were very nice about everything. All I have to do is get to Southampton in time for sailing tomorrow."

"Good. Turn that down or off, will you," Kent directed, nodding toward the television. "Unless you want to hear the rest of the news."

"Anything fascinating?"

"Lord, no!" He waited until she'd switched the set off and then went on. "I hope you're getting hungry because I put that frozen stuff in the oven fifteen minutes ago. That means you have time for a drink if you want one."

"It sounds good. Is your ankle any better?" she asked, noticing that he winced as he pushed back in the corner of the davenport.

"I think so. The swelling's gone down a little."

"You probably should still see a doctor," Barbara said, viewing him uneasily.

"It'll be all right in a day or so when I fly to Norway," he said, brushing her protest aside. "How about you? You look a little pale. Maybe you did too much running around today."

"I'm not tired at all," she snapped, wishing that she'd remembered to put on some new lipstick in the cab.

"Well, you'll feel better after a drink," he went on, ignoring her.

"I'm more interested in having something decent for dinner," she said, going into the tiny kitchen and opening the refrigerator.

"If you're worried about the salad—I've already fixed it," Kent said. "It's on the bottom shelf. There's a split of champagne there, too, if you'd like it—or scotch in the cabinet above."

Barbara decided that scotch on the rocks sounded like the least effort after noticing that he'd filled the ice bucket on the counter top. Apparently he wasn't a man to sit around and be waited on. Not only that, the salad he'd fixed looked delicious! She prepared a weak drink and went back to the living room, asking, "Would you like me to freshen yours before I sit down?"

"No, thanks. I just made it." He watched her settle on the other couch before adding casually, "Maybe I should have waited, but I wasn't sure when you'd be back."

So she needn't have worried, Barbara thought as she sipped her drink and reached for a cheese cracker from a dish on the table. If she'd been back earlier, they'd merely have watched the news on the BBC.

He nodded his thanks as she offered the dish to him. "Incidentally, you had a phone call about an hour ago."

Her eyebrows went up in surprise. "I wonder if anything's wrong at home."

He shook his head. "Not long distance. At least, not the way you mean. This was from Brighton—your friend, Derek Redmayne. He seemed a little puzzled—wasn't sure he had the right number."

That wasn't surprising since she hadn't given it to him, Barbara thought. Evidently he'd found some kind of reverse directory and tried his luck.

Kent seemed interested in the bottom of his glass as he swirled his drink. "It took a little while but finally he came right out and asked who I was."

A dreadful premonition stilled Barbara's hand on the point of selecting another cracker. "I see," she said in a cold, careful tone. "And what exactly did you tell him?"

"Well, I started to say we were sharing the flat and then I realized that he might not understand. I didn't want to go into a long explanation so I just said that I was a friend of yours and I'd give you the message when you came back later."

Her eyes narrowed. "How did he take that?"

"It's hard to tell with the British. They always sound a little stiff—even if they're giving you the time of day."

"Umm." She picked up a cracker then and chewed it thoughtfully. When Kent didn't say any more, she asked, "What was the message? Derek's message," she prompted as he still looked puzzled. "You're supposed to give it to me."

"Oh, that. Nothing vital. He was planning to be back in London ahead of time and wanted to meet you." Kent used his finger for a stirrer as he rearranged the ice cubes in his drink. "Naturally I told him that was out of the question because you wouldn't be here."

"Thanks very much."

Her sarcasm didn't go unnoticed. "Don't worry, he'll still be holding the fort when you come back. I even told him that I'd make sure you sent him a postcard from Norway."

"I hope he was suitably grateful."

"If he was, he did a good job hiding it, but I didn't mind. It'll do him good to be kept waiting." Kent consulted his watch, obviously considering the topic of Derek closed. "Right now there's a pretty decent sports wrapup on BBC before the soccer match."

"I'll turn it on," she said, getting to her feet. She'd already decided that Derek wasn't worth another argument, since it didn't matter whether he'd be in London waiting on her return.

"Aren't you going to watch this?" Kent asked, after she'd turned the television on and started to leave the room. "I don't want to drive you out."

"You haven't. I'm just going to try and serve

dinner. And since there isn't a dining room or eating space in the kitchen, it's apt to be informal."

"More than you imagine," he admitted. "There aren't any tray tables either."

"Then we'll pretend it's a picnic and unless the frozen chicken is better than I think it is—we may have to pretend it's eating."

"Never mind, we can always concentrate on the soccer match," Kent said, unperturbed. "Let me know if there's anything you want me to do."

Since he was engrossed in the television by then, Barbara ignored his offer. It made sense, because there wasn't room in the kitchen for two people—hardly enough space for one to get out the plates and cutlery.

Their main course of chicken bore a startling resemblance to its foil-wrapped relatives across the Atlantic, but it wasn't bad. Fortunately, the salad was excellent and the two French pastries which she'd gotten on impulse were good enough to cover the coffee, which tasted like pencil shavings.

Kent seemed more interested in his soccer match than the food, but nevertheless got to his feet when they were finished and insisted on carrying their dishes back to the kitchen.

"You should stay off that foot as much as you can," Barbara scolded. "Besides, it won't take me long to do the cleaning up and there really isn't room for two."

"Then I'll do it," he said, stacking his cup

and saucer beside hers in the sink. "It's easier for me than trying to make a bed, so if you wouldn't mind . . ." His voice trailed off as he looked at her inquiringly.

"You—mean you—want me to do it now?" Barbara stammered, caught off base by the request.

"Well, both of us have to get up early. I'll probably be gone by the time you leave for your train to Southampton." His voice was matter-of-fact and he kept his attention on the stainless steel sink.

"I didn't know you were going out, too."

"Business," he replied over his shoulder. "It just came up this afternoon. Don't worry, there won't be any last-minute trouble. I'll be at the dock when your ship arrives in Bergen or get word to you through the purser. Keep your fingers crossed for decent weather; calendar pictures look like the very devil in the rain and we can't stick around there long enough to wait for blue sky."

"Aside from praying for sunshine, what else am I supposed to do when I get there?" she asked, matching his businesslike tone as she hovered in the hall.

"Fill in the gaps for me. An attractive woman adds a lot to the picture of a fish market."

"It's nice to know we rate above the flounders."

"Even above the herring, so far as I'm concerned," he assured her. "I also need you to lean against a tree while you stare at that lakeside cottage where Grieg composed."

"You mean we'll get to go there, too?"

"I certainly hope so." He gave her an amused glance as he squirted soap in the sink. "And if you can hang onto the misty-eyed look that you have right now, you'll be worth my investment."

She looked ruefully back at him. "I certainly hope so. I'm beginning to feel guilty already."

"Then you can salve your conscience by letting me have a bed in the living room tonight. Since I have to be the first one out in the morning, I'd probably waken you if I traipsed through from the dressing room. The only thing is, that metal cot in there won't do much for your beauty sleep."

Barbara plunged in quickly before he could change his mind. "The cot won't bother me at all. I'd practically slept the clock around when you woke me this morning, so it won't matter." She crossed her fingers behind her skirt as she spoke, but it saved having to decline an offer of the other sofa bed in the living room. "I hope there's enough bed linen in the closet," she went on as if that were the only thing on her mind.

"There should be plenty. Janice doesn't usually miss on the details."

Just on her booking dates, Barbara thought grimly, but had enough sense not to mention it aloud. Instead she said, "Well, since you won't let me do any work in here, I'd better fix the beds."

She was aware that she sounded just like a den mother or the chaperone at a slumber party. Kent must have thought so, too, because he had an unnaturally solemn expression on his face as he said, "Good idea. I'll move my stuff into the living room once you're finished."

To think she'd wasted even one minute worrying about whether they should share the flat for the night, Barbara fumed as she reached into the armoire and yanked out sheets and pillowcases with angry abandon. If they had conducted many more conversations like that gem, she wouldn't even have to bother making the beds—Kent would be dozing off over the rinse water.

At least it was better than sleeping with a chair propped against the doorknob, she told herself defiantly, battening down on the conclusion that there must be a happy compromise in between.

She managed to keep such deplorable thoughts from her expression as she hauled off the slipcover on one of the divans and wrestled with making the bed. It was impossible to tuck the sheets and blanket in against the wall without sprawling across the top of the divan at the finish and that was how Kent found her when he limped back into the living room.

"You don't have to bother—I'll kick it apart in the first five minutes anyhow," he told her carelessly.

"Well, in that case, remember to do it with your good ankle," she said, sliding back off the bed as he perched on the end of the other divan to watch her. "Would you like two pillows?"

"If there are enough to go around." He watched her go back into the dressing room and come out carrying one of his bags. "Hey, I said I'd get those."

"The only thing you're supposed to do is—"

". . . keep my ankle up. I know," he finished impatiently.

"Then do it," she said, matching his exasperation. His other bag was much smaller and she brought it out to place it beside the first one.

"I'd better help you set up a cot in there," Kent said, pushing himself erect.

"I've already done it. Once I make it—everything's set." She gave him an uncertain glance. "I imagine you'd like to go to bed."

"At quarter to eight?" he asked, consulting his watch. "Isn't that carrying things a little far?"

She nodded reluctantly. "Well, I didn't plan to go to sleep," she confessed.

"What *did* you have in mind?"

"I could always read."

"Not in the dressing room unless you borrow a flashlight. That overhead light must be a good twenty-five watts. Do you play chess?" he asked, in sudden hope.

Barbara shook her head, not about to confess that her game level would put him to sleep even faster than the conversation.

"Well, that leaves television." He gestured toward the couch. "I wonder if they've already started the reruns over here."

It was either a German film classic with subtitles or a panel discussion on common market aims. They opted for the former and, twenty minutes later, Barbara was having trouble keeping her eyes open. She slipped out during a station break to change into tailored pajamas and a thigh-length robe and then went into the bath to brush her teeth.

"I'll leave you to it," she told Kent briefly when she passed back through the living room en route to bed.

He stared at her dispassionately and then nodded. Barbara could feel her cheeks getting red under his deliberate appraisal and told herself not to be foolish. The pajamas and robe were perfectly adequate—more than adequate by most standards. That gave her courage to say, "I hope you manage to get some sleep with that ankle."

He shrugged. "There's always aspirin if it's a nuisance. I'll try not to disturb you when I get up in the morning."

"Don't worry about it and you don't have to turn off the television," she added when he leaned over toward the dial. "If anything, that'll put me to sleep."

His smile appeared briefly. "I'd noticed. With programs like that, nobody has to buy sleeping pills. All they'd have to do is sell a tape of the movie at a drugstore."

Barbara smiled her agreement and disappeared into the dressing room, closing the door behind her. She'd thought about bidding him a proper farewell and then decided against it. Nothing was more embarrassing than to go through such a rigmarole and then meet over a cup of coffee in the morning. Although if she had anything to do with it, Barbara thought as she stretched out on her cot bed, she'd stay safely out of sight until Kent deserted the premises.

Unfortunately, she didn't remember her sensible decision when a series of noises awakened her in the middle of the night. The sound of something falling in the next room and a muttered expletive brought her to her feet in a hurry. She switched on the small light at the table next to her cot and tiptoed over to open the door, hovering uncertainly on the threshold.

"I should have known that would have brought you around." Kent spoke bitterly as he limped into the living room, carrying a glass in his hand.

"I wasn't sure who it was," she mumbled, a little disconcerted to find him wearing only the bottoms of his pajamas as he walked toward his tumbled bed. "It might have been somebody breaking in again."

"Didn't it occur to you that I would have heard anybody jimmying the front door?"

"Not if you'd taken a pain pill or a sleeping pill or something like that."

"I don't make a habit of doping myself at bedtime," he replied, his tone icy. "If you must know, I just got up to get a glass of water so I could swallow some aspirin. Unfortunately, I forgot about that damned electric kettle on the counter top."

"Is your ankle keeping you awake, after all?"

He let his glance sweep over her, suddenly

aware that the light behind her faithfully outlined her figure in her thin pajamas. "Let's say it's a contributing factor."

"Is there anything I can do?"

Kent must have heard the uncertainty in her voice, but it didn't soften his tone as he said forcefully, "Nothing other than get the hell back to bed. I'm a little old to have my hand held and I never did like Mother Goose." At her shocked withdrawn breath, he rubbed his forehead and said, "Forget it. I'm in a lousy mood. I'll try not to disturb you again."

"That's all right." Barbara knew she wouldn't leave the dressing room again even if she heard Godzilla roaring through Piccadilly just a block away. She risked another glance at Kent, aware of the breadth of his bare shoulders and chest even in the apartment's pale light. Although he hadn't moved, his presence seemed to surround her and invade the very fiber of her being. She took another deep breath and backed hurriedly away, adding, "I'll say good night, then—or is it good morning?"

Evidently he didn't think that inane comment was even worth an answer. The last glimpse she had before she closed the dressing room door was his definitely mocking gaze which told her that he'd managed to see through more than her pajamas—he'd successfully read her mind as well.

~§ 4 §~

When Barbara caught her first glimpse of Bergen's picturesque harbor four and a half days later, she felt a completely different person from the woman who had retreated from London. It wasn't until she'd presented her steamship ticket at dockside in Southampton that next morning and had been cordially welcomed aboard that she felt her dream vacation really was going to come true.

It was ridiculous to have doubted Kent's word, she realized then, except that it was hard to believe her good fortune. When she was informed that she would be sitting at the staff captain's table for the cruise, she gulped and sent up prayers that her limited wardrobe would see her through.

The young staff captain and his other table guests put her at ease during the first meal and, by the second, she was wondering why she'd ever harbored any doubts. A spell of blue skies had

added to the halcyon cruise life, giving an added
charm to the call at Edinburgh and later to the
glistening fjord scenery of Norway. The ship had
made its leisurely way through the magnificent
Sognefjord, finally anchoring at Flam so that passengers could enjoy the famous train climbing
dramatically up from the sea level to invade the
still snow-covered mountains. The combination
of cloudless sky with the sun shining on the jagged
peaks was a sight that Barbara knew she'd remember forever.

She'd been almost as fascinated the day before
on the North Sea crossing from Scotland. Instead
of the vast unbroken stretch of water she'd expected, their passage had been dotted with oil
platforms on either side of the ship. There was
almost constant helicopter traffic as well as new
rig crews being ferried in—plus a steady stream
of supply craft making their way both from Britain
and Norway. It had been the middle of the day
when an announcement came over the ship's public address system that all of the oil platforms
for the rest of the trip were Norwegian ones,
but Barbara noticed that only the flags were different. That evening, the staff captain had mentioned the billions of dollars invested by the two
countries.

"You would not believe the difference it has
made to our economy," he said in his accented
English. "Wait until you see the Shetland Islands
after our Bergen call—they've come alive again."

"Because of the oil?" Barbara asked.

"Just because of the oil," he said, nodding. "The power of it is almost unbelievable."

Such sobering thoughts were put to the back of her mind on the morning when the ship nudged up to the pier in Bergen. The weather was magnificent again, bathing the picturesque old town in bright sunshine that dispelled any thought of the frozen northland. Green hills surrounding the harbor with its neat red-roofed structures provided a blend of old and new, echoing the city's varied history. Looking over the bow of the ship as the officers brought her in to the pier, Barbara could glimpse the famous old Hanseatic houses where the merchants of the Middle Ages conducted their business. The pointed gables and tall buildings with narrow alleyways alongside led to secluded courtyards in the rear. The citizens of Bergen apparently were intent on preserving their history, but the traffic on the busy thoroughfare in front of the houses was strictly contemporary. So was the car ferry which was just then coming into the other side of the pier with passengers waiting on deck for speedy disembarkation.

Barbara shared their enthusiasm to view the city, but she was also strangely shy at the prospect of meeting Kent again—this time definitely on foreign ground. She stood on tiptoe by the railing, trying to see the entire length of the pier below as the stern line was secured and the forklift operator started shifting the gangway in place amidships. There were scattered groups of people along the dock, most of them calling and waving to friends and acquaintances on the promenade deck. Barbara searched carefully again and then drew a relieved breath because Kent's tall figure wasn't in sight. When the gangway was finally made fast, an announcement came over the public address system that the ship should receive customs and immigration clearance shortly. That gave her probably another ten minutes to decide if she should go ashore with the passengers already lining the stairway or if she should wait and be claimed. Like a misplaced parcel, she told herself, and then grinned reluctantly. It certainly wasn't any hardship to stay aboard for morning coffee and, in the meantime, she could change to a pair of low-heeled pumps and a decent "going ashore" outfit.

Back in her stateroom, she rummaged through her closet and settled on a silky houndstooth plaid with a pleated skirt that clung smoothly at the hips. The tones of royal and midnight blue were especially flattering, and a touch of azure shadow made her eyes worth a second glance. After a final look in the mirror, she made sure that she had her embarkation card and her traveler's checks and then went out, locking the stateroom door behind her. She detoured by the purser's office to see if any messages had been left for her and, on discovering that there hadn't, made her way to a lounge near the stern where she could sit in the sunshine while enjoying coffee and a sweet roll. It was so peaceful there with the splendid bird's-eye view of the Bergen water-front that she didn't hurry, content to enjoy the weather and the scenery at her secluded table.

"We'd just about given up on finding you."

Kent's familiar deep voice behind her made Barbara jerk with surprise and her death-grip on the sweet roll put a shower of flaky crumbs in her lap as she turned to greet him. "Oh, good morning." She managed to get the roll back on the saucer then and stood up, brushing her skirt free from crumbs. "I didn't mean to keep you waiting," she went on, wondering why he'd used the royal "we" unless he meant that the ship's crew had been in on the search for her, too.

"It isn't important." He put his camera case on the table and pulled another chair into the sunshine beside her. "That coffee smells good."

"It is. Everything that comes out of the dining room on this ship is delicious. My new waistline can testify to that," she said with a rueful grin. "Another week aboard and I'd be applying for a job as fat lady at the circus."

He cast a careless glance over her. "I think you'd be safe for another two weeks at least. Have you had a good time?"

"Marvelous. Everyone's been wonderful. Did you bring my pumpkin with you?"

"Your what?"

"Pumpkin." Her eyes twinkled. "Somewhere the clock must be striking midnight and this is too good to last. Especially since you seem back to normal."

One of his dark eyebrows climbed skeptically. "And how did you figure that out?"

"Well, you're scarcely limping at all so you must want to take the rest of the cruise. Especially with our flat out of commission. How's the roof coming along?" she asked, striving for a casual note.

"Fine, I imagine." When he saw her sudden frown at that, he added, "I didn't hang around to watch."

"Then you found a hotel?" she asked, before she realized that it was no affair of hers.

The same thought must have crossed Kent's mind, but he merely nodded and changed the subject. "Want some more coffee before we set out?"

"No, thanks—but you go ahead." She gestured toward the coffee bar set up in the lounge nearby. "I'll watch you drink it."

He glanced casually over his shoulder. "Unless I'm mistaken, it's already taken care of. I'll pull up another chair for Jan."

Barbara's cup clattered onto her saucer as she followed the direction of his gaze and saw Janice Carling coming toward them, followed by a steward carrying a heavy tray.

"Well, isn't this nice?" Jan said, pulling up at the table with the air of a woman who'd accomplished everything she'd set out to do. "Black coffee for you, Kent darling, plus a currant bun and I'll just have the coffee." She beamed at the young steward who was setting out the china in front of them. He appeared completely mesmerized by Janice and it wasn't any wonder, Barbara thought. Her erstwhile landlady looked as fresh as the Norwegian morning in a fuchsia cardigan suit elegantly trimmed in black braid. Some rose quartz earrings added a final pleasing touch to her outfit as well as calling attention to Janice's sleek hairstyle.

Barbara stared down at her own houndstooth plaid that had looked so nice a half hour earlier and decided it bore a distinct resemblance to sackcloth.

"And how are you liking your first look at Norway?" Janice asked her, once the steward was sent on his way and she'd subsided in a chair.

From her tone, she might have been one of the ship's hostesses and it was an effort for Barbara to give a polite reply. "Lovely. I didn't know you were planning a visit here, too."

"It was really spur of the moment, wasn't it, Kent?" She let her hand rest possessively on his tweed sleeve and smiled at him before going on to Barbara. "I decided I needed a break and when I heard that Kent was flying to Norway"—her hands went out in a graceful airy gesture—"that was all I needed."

Kent put his coffee cup carefully down in the saucer in front of him. "What Jan really means is that we shared an airplane on the way over this morning."

"Don't be so brusque, darling," the brunette

told him with an expressive grimace. "You make me feel dreadfully third-wheelish."

Barbara bit her lip so hard that she almost drew blood, wondering how many times Janice Carling had adopted that "little girl lost" routine. For her money, the woman was a card-carrying vampire no matter how well she played the ingenue role. Not that Kent would see it the same way, she thought as Jan's hand dropped on his sleeve again.

His very next words confirmed her fears. "You couldn't be a third wheel if you tried," he told the brunette with a slow smile, "but you still can't hang around when I'm trying to work this morning. And now if you're ready," he said, his tone going businesslike as he turned to Barbara, "we'd better get moving. I'd like to get out to Troldhaugen before the tour buses."

"You mean you're above organized group tours?"

"Don't be ridiculous. Anybody would know that you can't take decent pictures if there are people all around the place."

"You shouldn't be so rough on the poor girl," Jan told him with mock severity. "Just because you had to get up at the crack of dawn and missed some sleep. He's a bear when that happens," she confided, leaning over the table.

The only enjoyment Barbara got from that tidbit was seeing angry color surge over Kent's face and she thought fleetingly that he *did* react like a bear—one who'd emerged from hibernation with a nagging toothache.

"Well, if we've settled all that," he growled as he got to his feet, "I'd still like to get to work." He bent to take a last swallow of coffee and then wound the strap of his camera case around his wrist.

"Will this dress be all right?" Barbara asked as she stood, too. When he scowled uncomprehendingly, she added, "For the picture. Or would a sweater and skirt be better?"

Kent shook his head slightly as if to clear it. "You're fine that way. Let's go down this afterstairway to the gangway and miss the crowd amidships." He started to usher Barbara ahead of him and then turned to Jan as if he'd just remembered her presence. "What do you plan to do?"

"I hoped that you might buy me lunch after your picture session," she replied waspishly, showing that she didn't like being pushed out of the picture, both literally and figuratively.

He shook his head as he looked at his watch. "That would be cutting it fine. Best not to count on anything other than the flight out."

Barbara pulled to a stop beside him at the top of the stairs. "You mean you're not joining the cruise here?"

He shook his head, his features softening as he saw her perplexed face. "It doesn't fit into my schedule. We can get together when you arrive at the Shetlands tomorrow—I'll just be there ahead of you."

"We'll be there," Jan corrected. "I hope there's a decent hotel."

Barbara struggled to hide her disappointment at hearing Janice was going to be a permanent member of the party. The only satisfying aspect was that the brunette would far rather be enjoying the luxurious accommodations aboard ship than merely tagging along.

"If you want to go shopping," Kent was telling Jan as he led the way down the stairs to the lower decks, "we can share a cab to the center of town."

"Whatever you say." Despite the narrow stairs, she managed to hang onto his elbow. "At least I'll see you at the airport. And this time, don't cut it so fine. You know how I worry about things and what on earth would I do in the Shetland Islands by myself?"

"They aren't exactly the back of beyond these days," Kent told her and then seemed to remember that Barbara was behind them. "Are you okay?"

"Of course. Why wouldn't I be?"

He cast her a quick glance, obviously trying to figure out whether she was being sarcastic or really meant it. Barbara stared innocently back at him, fighting to subdue an impulse to trip them both when they started down the next flight of stairs.

By the time they'd reached the pier and found an empty taxi at the end of the big terminal, her annoyance had cooled. It was hard to maintain out-of-sorts behavior when the fascinating sights and smells of the Norwegian fjord capital were all around her. She was hardly aware of Jan's constant stream of conversation from the other corner of the seat because her attention was on the busy street outside. There wasn't nearly enough time to enjoy the old Hanseatic houses which she'd earlier seen from the ship, but the bumper-to-bumper traffic meant that the taxi had to go slowly past Bergen's world famous, open-air fish market. The place was thronged with people, but she could still appreciate the immaculate booths with colorful prawns and fish displayed on beds of ice and shielded from the sun by squares of canvas or vinyl. At the edge of the fish market there were fruit carts which served as attractive barriers to the flower markets just beyond.

Any hopes of Barbara's that they could linger in such an enchanted place collapsed when Janice informed Kent that she wanted to be put down at the largest department store in the city square. "At least I can amuse myself here while I'm waiting around for you," she announced as their cab pulled to the curb a few blocks later. "Don't bother to get out," she added and then gave him a fleeting kiss which barely missed its mark, landing on his cheek as he reached across to open the door for her. "I imagine I'll see you tomorrow," she told Barbara over her shoulder as a casual afterthought. "And do make sure that Kent gets to the airport on time for our flight."

Barbara could have replied but she settled for waving as Kent closed the door and gestured for the driver to move on.

A moment later, Kent showed that he hadn't missed her wistful looks out the window, saying, "If we have any time to spare after Troldhaugen and the old Stave church, we can come back to the fish market and let you wander 'round. Nobody should visit Bergen and miss out on that."

"I'd love to—and maybe we could look at the flowers, too." Barbara's irritation caused by Janice's presence disappeared as they drove down the busy streets and finally turned onto a four-lane freeway. And then it came back again as she noted a highway sign indicating that they were also on the road to Bergen's airport. "You certainly don't have to stay around town and entertain me when you're finished with your pictures," she said, the stiffness back in her voice. "I can find my way back to the ship without any trouble."

"That's always nice to know," he said, not bothering to hide his amusement as he shifted on the car seat and turned to look at her. "It's just too bad that you're sailing later today—Bergen's worth a lot more time. At least you'll enjoy seeing Grieg's haunts if you like his music."

"Oh, I do—tremendously," Barbara said, her annoyance fading quickly again under Kent's friendly manner. Damn the man, she thought wryly. He must know he could charm a woman without any effort at all. If only she could remember to remain cool and polite for the rest of their time together.

"Did you meet anybody interesting aboard?" he asked casually as the taxi turned off the freeway into a tree-lined street with older houses on either side.

"Well, everybody's been very nice. Unfortunately, there's no one from my part of the country at our table in the dining room so it's hard to form any lasting friendships—if that's what you mean."

"Sort of." He seemed to be choosing his words with care. "Sometimes you run into old acquaintances."

"Not in my circle." She gave him a rueful grin. "They go in more for rowboat rides in the park than North Sea cruises. You can't imagine what this will do for my social standing."

A moment later, their driver pulled off the bumpy road into a graveled parking lot. In broken English, he informed them that they would have to walk the rest of the way to Troldhaugen because of the narrow track.

"At least we seem to be between tour buses," Kent told Barbara as he helped her out of the taxi after making sure that their driver would wait for them. "With this weather, I hope to hell that I can get one usable picture." Then as he noticed Barbara choosing her way carefully down the rutted lane, he added, "Those shoes of yours aren't made for this gravel."

"Well, I didn't think a model in tennis shoes would sell calendars," she told him, keeping her tone level with an effort. From the way he was glancing over his shoulder just then, anybody would think he was hoping for a total stranger to come along and save him from having to make polite conversation. When he did nothing to break the lengthening silence between them, she let out an exasperated breath and made another try at a friendly atmosphere. "You'd never imagine that we're near a national memorial," she said determinedly. "With all these houses around, it looks just like an old-fashioned neighborhood from the Midwest—the kind you could find most anywhere."

He nodded and took a stab at following her lead. "Once we get to the top of the hill, you'll find a million-dollar view. Grieg bought Troldhaugen after he'd already received a fair measure of success, but he still used a little log cabin down by the water for most of his composing."

"What does Troldhaugen mean?" she asked, intrigued by the name.

"Troll Hill. When you see the house, you'll understand how the name fits. It's sort of a Hansel and Gretel setting in the middle of an enchanted wood."

"It sounds wonderful! Right now, though, it's so quiet we must have the place to ourselves," Barbara said as they trudged along up the gentle incline of the gravel trail.

There were trees on either side to provide a

dappling of shade so the sun's warmth wasn't oppressive. Most of the houses along the path were set in the middle of large lots and the combination of rolling lawns and birds fluttering overhead in the leafy branches brought a peace that made Barbara lower her voice instinctively. Even the crunching of their shoes on the gravel seemed abnormally loud.

Then suddenly they rounded a corner at the top of the hill and Grieg's home stood before them. It was a Victorian wooden structure with straight turn-of-the-century lines that fitted in perfectly with the austere beauty of his music. Past the tiny lawn and through the trees, sunlight glinted on the blue water below which surrounded the entire headland. Only a small dinghy marred its calm surface and when Barbara turned to face the house again, she was almost startled to find a smiling, middle-aged woman opening the front door in welcome.

"Volunteer hostess," Kent muttered, close to her ear. "Go on in and take the tour."

"But what about you—and the picture?"

"I'll be scouting out a decent location. When you're finished, come on down the path to the cabin by the lake. It's just over there," Kent said, jerking his thumb toward a corner of the lawn.

"Well, if you're sure . . ."

"I am. And take enough time to enjoy the manuscripts and sketches. How about money— do you have any kroner?" His hand went to his pocket.

"Yes, thanks. I changed some money aboard ship," she said, smiling.

"Okay. Go soak up the culture and I'll see you down below."

The twenty-minute tour was all that she could have hoped for and it was with reluctance that she left the Victorian landmark, thanking the Norwegian volunteer hostesses before she went outside to make her way down the steep, winding dirt path toward the lake. After the first fifty feet, she was tempted to take off her pumps and try it without heels, but the sight of a cabin roof through the trees made her realize she'd completed the steepest part of the trail. She came around a sharp bend on the path and found Kent braced against a tree trunk, camera in hand.

"Am I late?" she inquired breathlessly, almost slithering into him.

"Not enough to risk your neck," he said, keeping her at his side with a firm clutch on her elbow. "If you'd kept on at that rate, you'd end up in the water. How did you like the house?"

The last query came with barely a change of expression so Barbara decided that he couldn't be too annoyed with her. "It was tremendous—I enjoyed every minute of it," she said. "You could still feel the wonderful atmosphere in the rooms after all this time. I'm not surprised that Grieg and his wife chose to be buried out here since they loved the place." Her glance went down to the simple log cabin at the end of the path with its unhampered view of the water.

"That fits in, too. I'll think of Troldhaugen every-time I hear the *Peer Gynt Suite,*" she concluded softly.

There was a moment of silence and then Kent nodded. "Right. Well, I've taken a couple of pic-tures of the cabin from this angle that might do. Let's try one with you near the front step—partial profile and looking toward the water."

"All right." She felt a twinge of amusement when he frowned at finding he was still grasping her elbow, and released it with a brisk movement. Obviously he hadn't meant to maintain the con-tact, Barbara thought as she made her way down the remainder of the twisting path. In fact, he'd looked almost angry again. But why on earth had he bothered to meet her if she were only a source of annoyance?

She was still trying to figure that out as she reached the corner of the porch as he'd ordered. Ignoring a strong urge to peek in the window so she could see the composer's upright piano and work table, she turned to check her location for Kent's picture composition. He gestured her a few feet to the right and then signaled her to stay where she was.

She remained as still as possible, moving only when he finally called for her to try resting one hand against the tree trunk nearest the hut. Then, when he said, "Okay, that'll do it," she scooted up the steps for the quick look inside the cabin.

"You didn't have to hurry that much," he told her as she finally came back up the path to join him. "Our taxi will still be waiting. Go back down if you'd like and take your time."

She shook her head. "The path's too steep. Besides, I was able to see all I wanted. Actually, this whole morning has been unbelievable. I certainly never dreamed when you sprained your ankle that this would be the result."

"That's a devious female comment if I ever heard one," he said, sounding amused. "It doesn't matter though. You're here and frankly you look a lot more rested than when you left London."

"With the royal treatment I've gotten aboard ship, it's not surprising."

The sudden sound of voices at the top of the hill made Barbara shift her attention from the path and the next thing she knew she'd slithered off the loose shale and was clinging to a protruding branch on the steep drop-off alongside.

"Hang on, for God's sake," Kent ordered as he clamped down on her free hand.

"I'm hanging, but not for long," she panted, before he heaved her back onto the path.

In his anxiety, he used more force than necessary and she ended up against a tree trunk behind him, giving thanks that she wasn't nose-deep in its bark.

"Are you all right?" he wanted to know as she straightened, brushing herself down.

"Great, just great," she said somewhat grimly, wondering how she could appear any more inept in front of the man. And to think that she'd planned to impress him with her cool sophistication during the day! She glanced down the hillside to add wryly, "That first step's a dilly. I was almost back down at the cabin, after all."

"And if you hadn't stopped at the cabin, you could have ended up six feet under in the lake."

"That *did* occur to me." She brushed her hair back from her face. "I'm glad that you have quick reflexes."

His grin appeared momentarily. "After my episode at the zoo, I decided I'd better develop some. At least now we're even."

"For the moment." She sounded rueful as she surveyed their surroundings. "I'm not going to start bragging until we get to the top of the path. Unless you have other ideas."

His eyebrows drew together. "What do you mean?"

"Well, what other pictures are you planning? I can't think that you're furnishing me with a trip to Norway just for a five-minute session down there at the hut. *Nobody's* that generous."

For a moment, he looked disconcerted and then he shrugged, gesturing her ahead of him up the narrow path. "You're right. There are some other things on my schedule. Time's a factor, though. We'll try for the Stave church on the way back to town and then do the flower market if the weather cooperates."

They went up the rest of the path in silence and, once they reached the top, walked across to the gravel track they'd taken from the parking lot. It was still deserted as they trudged back toward their waiting taxi driver. An elderly golden retriever appeared suddenly from behind a hedge, barked once at them as if he felt it necessary, and then disappeared.

Barbara smiled and gestured toward the hedge. "He has to be the friendliest watchdog I've ever seen. It must be the atmosphere of this place— right now I wouldn't be surprised to find a troll around the next bend of the road. If it hadn't been for those volunteer guides who toured me through the house, I'd think we had wandered off the face of the earth."

She'd no sooner spoken than the sharp sound of a motorcycle cut through the quiet air. "That spoils the spell," Kent said, frowning, as the noise grew louder. "It must be one of the locals—nobody else would be coming flat out on this loose gravel."

Barbara nodded, thinking the cyclist must be almost upon them from the sound. An instant later he appeared from around a bend in the track and headed straight for them.

After that, everything merged into a terrifying blur. She only had time to see that the crouched rider wasn't altering his course so that he could pass them safely before she felt a hard blow on her back as Kent sent her sprawling onto the shoulder of the gravel track out of harm's way. As the motorcycle flashed by them, she let out another muffled shriek of pain when Kent fell on top of her. A split second later, they still lay in an untidy heap as the motorcyclist roared away without slackening his speed.

Kent was the first to move. He rolled off Barbara and sat up, shaking his wrist. "Are you all right?" he asked roughly, his voice not quite under control.

"I think so. This is getting ridiculous. It might have been better if I'd fallen in the lake." She pushed herself into a sitting position beside him and started to pull her skirt down. "Damn! My nylons took the count."

"The hell with them—how about your knees?"

She flexed her legs to find out. "Okay. What happened to your hand?"

"I fell on the camera and it didn't bend," he said grimly, giving the lens a perfunctory glance. "At least that isn't damaged."

"To quote you—the hell with the camera—how about your hand?"

He grinned reluctantly and tried flexing his fingers. "They work, too. I'd like to exercise them right now with a throttle hold on that creep's neck. He did his damnedest to hit us."

"The thought had occurred to me." She cast Kent a speculative glance. "You don't happen to work for the CIA in your spare time, do you?"

He eyed her warily. "What gives you that idea?"

"Every time I get within six feet of you, something happens," she told him. "Right now, I wouldn't be surprised to learn you were an only child."

"Pure coincidence," he told her. "Besides, I wasn't in the flat when it was ransacked. And, if we're being logical, I could point out that it works in reverse. We were together at the zoo and now this," he concluded with a grim look down the track where the motorcyclist had disappeared. "Are you sure some rejected suitor of yours isn't thirsting for revenge?"

"You've been watching too much television. I haven't had a rejected suitor since the third grade and he's now very happily married to my cousin." She went on before Kent could open his mouth. "They're hoping for a camping trip to the Tetons with their three children this fall if they can save enough money. Does that answer your question?"

"I guess so." He got to his feet, grimacing slightly, and bent to help her up. "Maybe this creep just hates tourists. There was some grass on your skirt." The last came after she gave a nervous jump as he brushed her derriere with the back of his hand.

"I see." She felt color flood her cheeks, aware that she'd overreacted. "Maybe we'd better just go back to the ship—I can't walk around town with my nylons in ribbons."

He was still watching her closely. "Do you want to?"

"Go back?" She dropped her glance and

brushed ineffectually at the front of her skirt. "Of course not. I hate to waste a minute of this day."

"Then there's no need to," he said, as if he'd just made up his mind. "You can buy some nylon hose at that department store where we deposited Jan. Afterwards, we'll walk down to the flower market. It isn't far."

"That sounds great," she said, managing not to limp as they started down the path again toward the parking lot where they'd left their taxi. "Let's just hope that our driver's still waiting or that walk may be longer than you planned."

"We'll be okay." He slung the camera strap over his shoulder and took out a small notebook from his hip pocket with some difficulty, making a note in it as they walked along. "Picture captions," he explained, intercepting her interested glance. "Can't tell who's running without a program."

Her lips twitched at his terse explanation and then her smile appeared as he struggled to replace the notebook in his pocket. "That's a pretty tight fit."

"Don't I know it! There's nothing like landing on a loose-leaf notebook when you hit the dirt. I'm going to have some interesting bruises tomorrow."

"Then you'd better let me help in case that maniac comes back," she told him, taking the notebook from his fingers and putting it in her handbag.

For a moment he looked undecided and then he shrugged, asking, "Sure you have room for it?"

"I could hide two or three of Mr. Grieg's trolls in there and still have room left over." She held out her purse as evidence. "Of course I get a little lopsided after a trip."

"In that case, I won't argue."

"I just wish that I'd thought to put an extra pair of panty hose in, as well," she said with another rueful look at her legs. "These are such a mess, I really should go back to the ship instead of shopping in town."

"That's just wasting time." He took a quick look around the quiet lane and then turned back to her. "Take them off here. There's nothing wrong with going into a department store bare-legged."

"But I can't—not with you—" She stopped stammering as he merely looked annoyed and turned his back. "Okay, but I hope that nobody's peering through the hedges at us," she muttered as she shed her shoes and raised her skirt to yank down her ruined panty hose.

"On a bikini beach, you wouldn't even rate a second glance. Of course, I can't say for sure," he continued blandly, ostensibly intent on a gray water bird that was swooping over the tops of some nearby trees, "since it would be hearsay evidence."

"I imagine you're well acquainted with the bikini beaches, though." She shot him an annoyed glance as she peeled off her hose and stuffed them into her purse.

"That's not surprising—in my job I travel a lot." He folded his arms over his chest in a gesture of resignation. "If you don't hurry up, the tour buses will be arriving and you'll find yourself on their itinerary."

"I'm almost ready." Barbara didn't try to hide the impatience in her voice as she struggled to get her shoe on.

"So I see." He turned and gave her another cursory glance. "You'll do. Nobody pays attention to green knees these days."

"The only way I could get rid of them would be to spit on my handkerchief and I'd hate to shock your inner sensibilities," she told him, starting off down the track again.

"You'd be surprised how much it takes to shock me," he replied conversationally. "Especially my inner sensibilities. I thought I'd gotten that across before this."

Her eyebrows rose. "I can't tell whether you're bragging or apologizing."

"And I don't know what the hell we're talking about. Are you sure you aren't suffering from a slight concussion?"

"Positive." She rubbed her derriere instinctively. "My head is the only place that's undamaged."

He frowned down at her. "I'm sorry about that. I must have come down on you pretty hard, but it all happened so fast."

"And if you hadn't reacted the way you did, I'd be complaining about a lot more than a few bruises by now." She smiled engagingly. "A case of green knees has made me forget my manners. Did I thank you for . . ."

". . . landing on top of you like a sack of potatoes?" He grinned in response—that slow grin that made his eyes crinkle at the corners and did such devastating things to her insides. "I think you might be forgiven for overlooking it. My God!" he went on conversationally as they rounded the bend of the track and could see the parking lot in front of them. "There are miracles, after all—our driver's still waiting. Hey, what are you doing?"

The last came when Barbara slowed her steps and fell in behind him. "If you *must* know, I'm trying to stay out of the limelight until I can get cleaned up," she muttered.

"Don't worry—the only thing he'll be concerned about is whether I brought enough traveler's checks if we go back by way of the church."

As it turned out, getting to the Stave church involved a fairly lengthy detour which did add to the amount on the meter. The taxi had to bump along another dirt track before they finally came upon the oriental-looking structure in a sylvan setting almost as pretty as Grieg's Troldhaugen. Only this time, the architecture of the wooden church would have fitted more easily into Malaysia or Thailand with its exotic silhouette. Barbara stared at it wide-eyed and then when

Kent made no move to get out of the car, she asked, "Aren't you going to take a picture? There aren't any other visitors to get in the way."

He leaned forward on the seat to peer through the window before sitting back and shaking his head. "The light is all wrong. I should have been here earlier. Oh, well, there'll be other times. Besides, there might be something good at the flower market that will provide a change. I'm inclined to go overboard on buildings and ruins." Glancing across at her, he went on with scarcely a pause, "Want to tour this or are you satisfied with a long distance view?"

He kept his tone light, but Barbara decided that he really didn't want to spend any extra time at the church. Probably he couldn't risk missing his plane or meeting Jan, she thought with a twinge. She was careful to keep her voice noncommittal as she replied, "This'll do, thanks. I'm all for another look at the flower market."

Fifteen minutes later, after they stopped at a bank so that Kent could cash a traveler's check, they were back at the city center in front of the main department store. Their driver insisted on shaking hands with both of them and wished them a pleasant stay in his broken English before driving off.

"You must have made his day," Barbara said with amusement as Kent came up beside her to hold the store door for her. "That stack of kroner you handed over looked big enough to settle the national debt."

"Well, he did wait for us and he struggled to

keep his glance off your legs when he let us out of the cab. God knows what he'll tell his wife when he goes home tonight."

"Probably that a couple of crazy Americans were rolling around in the shrubbery before lunch," Barbara said somewhat bitterly as they paused just inside the front door of the big department store. "You don't happen to know the word for hosiery in Norwegian, do you?" At his wry look, she smiled and said, "Never mind. I'll nose around. Do you want to come along or are you one of those men who turn pale at lingerie counters?"

"Maybe this is a good time to check it out." He steered her around two formidable Norwegian matrons who were taking up most of the aisle. "It looks promising back in that corner beyond the cosmetics."

Barbara discovered that he was right once again. Far from being embarrassed by feminine fripperies he corralled a young saleswoman and managed a dialogue that included a few English nouns, a great many gestures, and still more laughter before Barbara was given a package of panty hose.

"But everything written on this is French," she protested, trying to figure out the graph on the back of the package. "Are you sure it's the right size?"

Kent took the package from her and studied it solemnly. "I think so. How much do you weigh?"

She snatched it back. "It's none of your affair.

Honestly, nothing is sacred as far as you're concerned."

He grinned, unabashed, while the young saleswoman watched them intently. "Why don't you just go and put them on while I settle the financial side?"

"There's no reason for you to pay for my stockings." Barbara was rummaging in her purse trying to find her wallet as she spoke.

"Why not? After all, I was the one who came down on top of you by the roadside." He paused when the eavesdropping saleswoman drew in a pleased, shocked breath at that disclosure.

Evidently she understood far more English than she let on, Barbara decided. The way things were going, another Norwegian household would be regaled with spicy news of visiting Americans when the workday was over.

"I'll go put them on," she told both Kent and the saleswoman in the most dignified tone possible.

"Can you find the ladies' room?" he wanted to know.

"If I can't, I'll stand at the foot of the escalator and beat my breast—like Solveig bemoaning her fate when Grieg let the tenor interrupt her best aria."

Kent's eyebrows rose. "So I asked a stupid question . . ."

"Pliss?" Clearly this was beyond the saleswoman's English for Beginners and she didn't want to miss anything.

Barbara said, "Just pay the girl," to Kent before she started off.

"Wait a minute . . ."

His call stopped her before she'd gone more than a few feet and she glanced over her shoulder.

"Where do I meet you?" he wanted to know.

For the first time, he looked like a man who wasn't in control of everything and everybody. The thought warmed Barbara's heart and her smile was a little more kindly. "How about the bottom of the escalator? Fifteen minutes?"

"Right. I'll be there."

When Barbara met him as planned, she was glad that she was looking almost her best once again. Kent's glance lingered at her ankles and he grinned, obviously approving his purchase. "I may hang out my shingle as a professional shopper. Of course, it helps to have a pair of legs like yours to work with. Something tells me I've been taking pictures of the wrong—"

"Watch it," she interrupted.

His grin widened, obviously not disconcerted in the least by her warning. "I was just going to say that I'd been overlooking some of your more obvious assets."

"Umm. Such as?"

"Your splendid talent for conversation," he said, taking her elbow to steer her toward the store entrance. "How would you like to display it over a cup of coffee down by the flower market?" His expression sobered suddenly as he looked down at her by his side. "There are things we should discuss."

Her own upward glance was eloquent. "Such as why we were the target of that motorcyclist this morning? And don't tell me that it was an accident."

"I wasn't about to." He pulled open a heavy glass front door and followed her out onto the crowded sidewalk which fronted the pleasant town square. "Want to walk? It's only four blocks and downhill."

"I wouldn't mind if it were all uphill." Her voice quavered suddenly as he took her hand and pulled it into the crook of his arm. "A visit to Norway may be old hat to you, but I'm still counting my blessings."

He steered her around a young mother wheeling a stroller down the middle of the sidewalk before asking, "Even with everything that's happened?"

"Well, I can't pretend that I wouldn't have preferred a nice quiet day out at Troldhaugen," she admitted. "On the other hand, if that cyclist had really meant to get rid of us, there wasn't anything to keep him from coming back and trying to finish the job. Was there?" Her last query came when Kent stared deliberately ahead, as if only intent on strolling down the sunny sidewalk, enjoying storefront displays.

"I shouldn't think so," he said finally. "Unless he was afraid he might be recognized."

"By you?"

He did lower his glance then and she wondered how she could have ever thought that his expression had softened. At that moment, his gray eyes were as bleak and formidable as the waters of the North Sea that lapped the fjords. "That's what I wanted to talk about."

There wasn't any more conversation after that until they reached a pleasant coffeehouse with some tables and chairs out on the sidewalk. By then, they were at the bottom of the street so they could view the markets and the city's busy inner harbor. All about them were shoppers coming from the flower market laden with pansy and petunia bedding plants to stock their home gardens. Their lighthearted laughter showed that they didn't have anything serious on their minds and, for an instant, Barbara envied them before her common sense returned. It was a relief to have Kent decide on a moment of truth—although from his grim look it was obvious that he wasn't looking forward to it.

"Want to try a cream cake with your coffee?" he asked absently when they'd settled at a small round table near the corner of the restaurant enclosure and a waiter approached.

"Oh, no—thanks. All I've done on the ship is eat."

"Well, at least join me in a croissant. I can't remember the last meal I had without watching a clock," Kent said mildly after he'd given their order and the man had gone to fill it.

"You don't look like a man who's having a

riotous holiday," she agreed after putting her big purse at her feet and trying to settle back in her chair like a woman with nothing on her mind. "On the other hand, I don't really know you well enough to tell. Maybe you're one of those energetic souls who doesn't believe in vacations." She stared at him a moment longer and then burst out exasperatedly, "I wish to heaven that you'd tell me what's going on! Honestly, I've regressed to biting my nails. The next thing, I'll be buying a security blanket instead of picture postcards!"

"As bad as that?"

"You're darned right—" she broke off again when she saw amusement flicker over his stern mouth. "I don't really see anything funny about dodging mad motorcyclists—"

He put up an authoritative palm to stop her in midsentence as the waiter approached with their coffee and croissants. "I'm sorry about that," Kent said when they were alone again, "but I'd rather not attract any more attention than necessary. Want some butter and jam?"

"No, thank you." Barbara managed to take a sip of coffee without lowering her defiant chin.

Kent waited until she'd put her cup down and then reached across the table to capture her hand under his. "Look, for the first time since I've met you—I'm beginning to believe that we're on the same side in this thing so don't freeze me out. There isn't time to have a fight. Besides, you don't give a man a fair chance."

"I don't know what you mean," she said, yielding slightly but still managing frost around the edges of her voice.

"Then you haven't looked in a mirror lately." He took a swallow of coffee himself and seemed intent on tearing off a piece of croissant without getting crumbs on the table. "That's why I thought you were a little too good to be true when you showed up at the flat. Instead of a red herring, I thought they were trying their luck with a redhead."

She put up her hand and brushed back a strand from her face. "My hair's not red—it's brown."

"Not when there's a Norwegian sun shining on it," he assured her. "And your temper definitely goes with a copperknob."

"That's not surprising . . . you can be the most exasperating, stubborn, uncommunicative . . ."

Surprisingly, a look of satisfaction came over his face as her list of adjectives lengthened. When she finally ran out of breath, he said, "Definitely not the Mata Hari type. You should be cozying up instead of reading me the riot act."

"Like Janice Carling?" The accusation slipped out before Barbara could stop it, and the swift ascent of his eyebrows showed that he recognized a jealous remark as fast as the next man.

"Exactly," he replied. "But then she has to make a living and right now she thinks I'm ready for the plucking."

"*You* are." A frown twisted Barbara's forehead. "Do photographers make that much money?"

"I don't," he said with great patience, "but my stepfather's another story."

She stared at him, uncomprehending. "What does your stepfather have to do with all this?"

"Well"—Kent took another bite of croissant and chewed reflectively—"to start with—it's his flat in London."

Her eyes widened. "You mean the one that's mine—or yours?" She swallowed and started again. "It's his?"

It only took a second or two for Kent to sort out her gibberish. He grinned and said, "That's the general idea."

"Well, he might take the trouble to get his bookings straight after this. I hope you tell him the next time you see him."

"In all fairness—it wasn't his fault. As he didn't even want to rent the flat in the first place but . . ."

"You persuaded him," Barbara finished.

He stared at her. "I didn't know that you read crystal balls in your spare time."

"If I did, I wouldn't have left home," she replied, not in the least put off by his manner. "And I certainly wouldn't be here hanging on your every word."

"Is that what you're doing?"

"Yes, and your explanation's taking an awfully long time if you're in as big a hurry as you claim."

For a moment, his expression darkened. Clearly he wasn't accustomed to women who spoke their mind so frankly and Barbara drew in her breath, wondering if she'd gone too far.

"In that case," he said, keeping his tone carefully level, "maybe you'd better tell me what you want to know."

"All right. Why did you care about renting the flat? You aren't over here very much, are you?"

"A couple times a year." Kent drained his coffee cup and put it back in the saucer. "Actually, I wanted to do Janice a favor. She was short of money and it was a chance for her to make an easy commission. Philip—my stepfather—only used the flat when he came to town for meetings. The rest of the time it was empty unless I had a business trip to London. I'm sorry that you got involved."

Some men would have said they were glad it had happened, because otherwise they wouldn't have met, Barbara thought, but Kent wasn't one of them. Just then, he was surveying her with polite interest, probably wishing he could check his watch without letting her know. And it was mostly her fault, she reminded herself; she shouldn't have been so abrasive in playing the independent woman. Somewhere along the line, she'd forgotten that courtesy was still the best way. She drew in a deep breath and told him frankly, "I'm not sorry. And I was lying when I said that about not leaving home. I can't pretend that I like dodging motorcycles, but—" She gestured helplessly. "You know what I mean."

The smile came back to his gray eyes again. "Since confessions are in order, I'd better admit that I'm not in the habit of giving up my cruise tickets either. And now that we've gotten that out of the way—tell me what you know about North Sea oil."

If he'd asked what she thought about trying to stop a horde of lemmings from plunging into the icy waters of the harbor, she couldn't have been more surprised. "Are you serious?" she got out finally.

"Very much so." He rubbed his forehead tiredly. "From the looks of things, North Sea oil is the reason for the break-in at the flat. Also why you had to take that second nosedive this morning."

"But I don't know anything about North Sea oil. You can't think that . . ." Her voice dropped as another thought occurred to her. "Wait a minute. Maybe I don't know anything, but what about you?"

He held up his hands in protest. "Pure as driven snow. Unfortunately, it's a little harder to prove my case. My stepfather—"

"You mean he's connected with the North Sea project?" she asked, unable to contain her curiosity.

"I thought you were complaining about how long this explanation was taking," he said, trying to hold onto his patience.

"You're right." She held up her palms in apology. "You might as well know that I read the endings of books first, too. I can't wait to find out what happens."

"Well, I suggest that you stay out of this plot

from now on. That's why it'll be a good thing
if we part company as soon as I get you back
to the ship."

"Wait a minute—you're skipping the juicy
parts," she complained. "Like why they're gunning for your stepfather. Has he been dealing
off the bottom or absconding with the company
funds?"

"Good God! What kind of books do you
read?"

Kent sounded so affronted that Barbara hurried
to explain. "Well, you must admit that whoever-
it-is is playing pretty rough. I just thought that
maybe your stepfather was a . . ."

As she searched for a diplomatic word, Kent
supplied it. "Dastardly villain? Hardly. He's a
'backbone of the empire' type plus being a nice
guy as well."

"Then, why all this?"

"Because, my dear girl, he's in a government
ministry that deals with oil exploration in this
part of the world. My guess is that a lot of people
want to find out what effect their latest discovery
is going to have on the world market."

His explanation was surprising enough to make
Barbara ignore that casual "my dear girl" comment. "Oil exploration," she murmured and
shook her head. "That's big money. Really big."

"And big stakes for everybody concerned.
That's why it's safer for innocent onlookers like
you to stay on the sidelines."

Some of the facts that had been bothering her

fell into place with abrupt, disturbing significance. "So that's why you sent me on this cruise," she said, fixing him with a fierce look. "You wanted me out of the way."

He rubbed his jaw with his thumb and took his time about answering. "That's only partly true. I wasn't about to hobble around shipboard with my ankle and I *did* need a model."

She gave him a pitying smile. "I'm sure with a little more rehearsal, you could make that sound a lot more convincing. But it doesn't matter," she added when he opened his mouth to protest, "I still can't make head nor tail of the confusion over the flat."

"That's easy. Philip had been staying there while he was attending a series of meetings in London. After that, he knew that I was arriving, but we didn't get around to telling Janice about it. That's how the mixup occurred when you came to town—" He broke off in midsentence when Barbara held up her hand. "Now what?"

"Let's go back to Janice. I can understand all that about the double booking, but is she involved in the seamier side or just along for fun and games?"

For an instant, Kent was disconcerted and then rallied visibly. "You don't miss much, do you?"

"I seem to have missed practically everything up until now," Barbara commented with some bitterness. "And you still haven't answered my question."

"To be honest, I'm not sure of the answer. Jan had the misfortune to marry a twenty-four carat jerk and it took a while for her to divorce him. She still hasn't been able to break him of the habit of reappearing whenever he needs money. The damnable part is—if he doesn't get it, he roughs her up. Naturally, he's very sorry afterwards."

"But that's—that's terrible!"

"I agree with you one hundred percent and I've tried to convince her to shove him in the nearest manhole if she sees him coming." Kent pushed his saucer away and bunched his napkin beside it. "She's been sticking to me like glue these last few days." His expression was cynical. "I don't believe my magnetic personality rates such devotion."

Barbara shot him an appraising glance under half-closed lids and wondered what he'd say if she told him he was crazy. It was more than possible that the brunette was simply protecting her future interests in the matrimonial stakes. Finally she asked, "What do you think is on her mind?"

"I'd guess that her ex has found a way to get paid for any information he can gather on Philip's project. Jan knows my stepfather and she has a passkey to the flat. It's possible that she left it out at home and her ex-husband had a duplicate made. The fact that the break-in came when it did makes me think that Jan didn't know about it. 'Whoever-it-was' probably thought the place was empty. It was a good chance to check and see if Philip had left anything of interest lying around."

"And all they found was me sleeping off jet

lag." She shuddered. "I'm glad that I didn't wake up."

"So am I. This way, you're still safe."

"But what about this morning?"

"I told you." Kent signaled their waiter for the check and reached for his wallet when it arrived. "I'm ninety percent sure that it's me they're gunning for now." He put down some notes and thanked the waiter before saying to Barbara. "What about a quick trip across the street to the flower market?"

"But if you're serious, you shouldn't be traipsing around as a prime target," she protested, getting slowly to her feet as he stood up and waited by the table.

"Why not? I certainly don't plan to hibernate. Besides," he went on calmly, taking her elbow as they came to the curb and threaded their way through the traffic at the intersection, "my stepfather's on an inspection trip in the Shetlands now and his ministry will make public all the information on the new field in the next day or so. After that, our friends will have to find some other business investment."

She pulled up as they reached the far curb, ignoring an overweight man who almost cannoned into them.

"That's not the way to survive abroad," Kent said, pulling her out of the way, his glance alive with laughter.

"I'm sorry," she began automatically and then forgot such trivia as she said, "I didn't know you were going to the Shetlands to see your stepfather."

"So I gathered this morning. You looked extremely disapproving when you heard about it. Which shows that you shouldn't let your imagination go galloping until you know the facts. What looks best to you? Roses? Or maybe some of those exotic lilies?"

The last was added with scarcely a pause as he walked her over to the nearest canvas-covered flower stand. There were rows and rows of potted petunias and geraniums on the ground around them, but containers of roses and lilies plus violets and carnations were more carefully displayed on counters out of the sun.

Barbara took a deep sniff of the carnations in front of her and then her attention was caught by some more delicate blossoms nearby. "Freesias," she said in delight. "Imagine finding them here!" She bent to sniff ecstatically again. "I've always thought that the yellow ones have the most fragrance. Aren't they wonderful?"

"I'll take your word for it," Kent said, reaching down to extract two big bunches of yellow freesias and handing them to the smiling flower seller for wrapping. "At least you'll have something pleasant to remind you of Bergen once you get back on shipboard."

Barbara's face fell. "You mean that I should stay aboard until we sail? That this is . . ."— she gestured around her—"this is it?"

Kent's expression hardened at her obvious disappointment. "I'm sorry, but I think you'd be foolish to take any more risks. I'll have to leave you on your own in a few minutes and, after this morning"—he shrugged graphically—"I don't like the odds."

The flower seller was obviously puzzled at the solemn turn of events and he muttered something in Norwegian as he handed over the freesias, grinning broadly a moment later as Kent gave him a note and waved away the change.

"Thank you for the flowers," Barbara said dutifully as she clutched the fragrant armful. "And the coffee, too."

Kent burst out laughing. "You sound like a ten-year-old after a birthday party."

"Well, I don't feel like one," she retorted, determined not to rise to his teasing. It was all very well for him to casually give orders for the rest of her day, but quite another to follow them unreservedly. The easiest policy would be to do as he suggested and reboard the ship—then decide herself whether she'd stay there until they sailed. "Do you want to walk back to the pier with me or shall I take a taxi?" she asked him with a cool smile.

Kent's eyes narrowed—as if surprised at her easy acquiescence. "The walk shouldn't take long and it seems a shame to waste this sunshine."

Her shrug was a masterpiece. "Whatever you say. You're the boss."

"I wonder what it is that makes me . . . ,"

he began and then obviously changed his mind about finishing the sentence.

"Makes you what?"

"Nothing. It isn't worth another argument." His tone was almost terse and he took her elbow in a firm grip, turning her out of the flower market down a walkway leading through the colorful outdoor fish market. The displays were models of cleanliness with the fish atop tables of crushed ice which in turn were shaded by lean-to roofs. "Can I interest you in a package of prawns?" Kent asked, striving for a light tone. "They tell me they're delicious."

"I'm sure they are, but the room steward might object to finding them in my closet." She hovered over an attractive display as a stall owner smiled. "Apparently half the ship's crew brings them back for a feast. My waiter said Bergen's one of the favorite ports because of this fish market."

"And here I'm rushing you back to the ship without even a chance at a smorgasbord lunch. They have wonderful specialties like boiled pollack or broiled Norwegian salmon served with whipped sour cream and horseradish," Kent said, casually starting toward the sidewalk, leaving her little option but to follow. "We'll have to make up for it at the Shetlands."

"Do they specialize in seafood, too?" Barbara asked dryly. "I thought it was mainly oil wells these days. With cardigan sweaters as a sideline."

"You sound like an expert. We can check out

the cardigan market tomorrow and see if you're right," he said casually. "Maybe those shetland sweaters are the real reason that Janice is so anxious to go along."

"I'm sure you're the expert on that," Barbara replied, trying not to let her annoyance show. Apparently Janice Carling's various failings and ex-husbands didn't really bother him at all. Certainly not enough to shake off such an eye-catching traveling companion. And undoubtedly a most cooperative one, she told herself.

"Oh, I wouldn't go so far as to say that," Kent said, slowing his pace in front of an attractive gift shop once they'd left the market area and were headed toward the block of old Hanseatic houses again. "Looks as if they have some attractive things in here. Wouldn't you like a souvenir to go along with those flowers?"

She allowed herself a quick survey of the attractive knitted ski mittens and carved wooden trolls before shaking her head. "No, thanks."

"If it's money that's bothering you—" He broke off at her angry flashing glance.

"Look, you've already given me the cruise tickets," she said through a tight jaw. "You don't have to do any more. I'm perfectly capable of managing without a subsidy from here on."

"There's no need for you to take it like that . . ."

"Then let's forget about it." She managed a quick glance at her watch as if a thought had just occurred to her. "If we get a cab, I can still

make lunch aboard. That way, you won't have
to waste any more time."

Kent made a token effort of saying, "I wouldn't
exactly call this wasting time, but it's up to
you."

His words would have been more convincing
if he hadn't been looking up and down the busy
boulevard for an empty taxi even as he protested,
Barbara decided and clamped down hard on her
lower lip to steady it.

As luck would have it, there was a cab stand
at the very end of the block, and in no time at
all she found herself ensconced on another black
vinyl seat headed back for the dock. She stared
stonily ahead, all set to show her disdain if Kent
commented on the historic steeple of the twelfth-
century St. Mary's church as the car bowled along
and sneaked a surprised sideways glance when
he didn't even mention it. Instead, he, too, was
staring at the back of the driver's head as if it
rated his complete attention. Certainly he didn't
bother to remark on King Haakon's Hall which
she'd read about, and ignored the local car ferry
that was leaving a nearby pier. A few minutes
later the taxi braked alongside the security man
guarding the entrance of the cruise ship pier, but
Kent stayed immobile, his arms crossed over his
chest like some medieval deity who didn't like
his lot in life. And she probably looked just as
disagreeable, Barbara decided. The cab driver
must wonder what was wrong with two people
who were interested only in the dusty interior

of his car when there was a beautiful sunlit world beyond the windows.

At that moment as they waited, the driver's attention was focused on a large ship which was completing its docking at the other side of the pier from the cruise ship. Encountering Barbara's glance in the rear vision mirror, he gestured toward the ship, saying in heavily accented English, "First crossing of the season. Coming from Newcastle each week. Nice, yah?"

"Very nice."

A frown marred Barbara's brow as she tried to remember where Newcastle was—but even as she started to inquire, Kent said tersely, "England. Near the Scottish border," showing that he was reading her thoughts again.

Before she could comment on it, the cab started moving as the guard waved them through the gate.

Kent was out on his side as soon as the taxi stopped near her cruise ship's gangway, gesturing for the driver to remain where he was. "I'll need you to take me back to town," he said and went around to open Barbara's door.

She stepped out without touching his offered hand and stood clutching her flowers. "Thank you again—," she began, only to have Kent cut in roughly.

". . . for helping to almost get you killed. You don't really have to be that polite," he said, rubbing the back of his neck as if it had developed a nagging ache.

Barbara kept a noncommittal expression on her face, deliberately ignoring the tired lines she suddenly noticed at the corners of his eyes. Damned if she'd start feeling sorry for him. Especially when he'd probably lost all that sleep larking around with Janice Carling. If he needed sympathy, he'd get a full measure of it from her. That thought helped her to keep the ice in her tone as she said, "In that case, I won't bother. You needn't come any farther with me. I can find my way up the gangway without any help."

"Then I hope you can find your way down it tomorrow in the Shetlands. And you'd better dig out something warm to wear for the pictures there—just make sure that it's feminine-looking."

"I thought you were going to meet your stepfather."

"That doesn't have anything to do with taking pictures later on." He gave her an annoyed look. "You'll still have a job to do so don't get any ideas to the contrary."

"Don't worry," she said, trying to sound as if she'd never thought differently, "I'm perfectly prepared to do my part. Now, if there isn't anything else on your mind—I'd like to get aboard." It was hard to stare haughtily down her nose at him when he towered over her by a good ten inches, but she managed.

He reached out and caught her elbow in a steely grip when she started to walk away and dragged her roughly back against him.

"What do you think you're doing—" she stuttered.

His grip tightened, cutting her protest in midsentence. "I just remembered something else on my mind," he said angrily, "since you've been kind enough to remind me."

"That's all very well, but—"

"I've decided that we both might as well get something to remember out of this day. At least you've managed a bunch of flowers," he continued in that ominous tone which made her eyes widen, "so I'll take something, too. God knows, I've earned it by this time!"

With that, he tipped up her chin with his free hand and bent to cover her mouth in a rough, possessive kiss that sent her senses reeling.

She forgot all about the bustle of people by the gangway, the waiting taxi, even the bus nearby unloading passengers from the morning tour. It finally took the blast of the ship's whistle from the other side of the pier to restore her to reality and she pushed back just far enough to breathe again as she rested against his crisp shirt front.

The therapy session didn't last long; she was clinging to his shoulders, still wondering whether the thundering heartbeats were hers or came from Kent's broad chest, when he stepped back and put her at a safe distance from him.

"I'm sorry about that," he said, getting the words out from a tightly clenched jaw. "I hadn't planned on it happening."

If he'd suddenly shoved her into the big bin

of crushed ice that a longshoreman was wheeling by them just then, Barbara couldn't have been more shocked. It was one thing to be kissed unexpectedly and come up reeling in pleasant delirium, but when one of the participants looked distinctly annoyed and announced to all and sundry that it was a big mistake—the rainbow colors turned to stark black and white.

That left only one role for her to play if she didn't want to appear the complete idiot. She managed to put a bland expression on her face as she stared past his ear. "I've never known such a man for taking things seriously," she said in a light, uncaring tone. "What's a kiss now and then? Obviously you haven't been aboard a cruise ship lately."

"I didn't know that I was so far behind the times," he snarled back, not uplifted by that bit of news. "It's too bad that we don't have a little longer so that you can tell me about your adventures on the high seas."

"Who knows? Maybe by our next port of call, there'll be more to tell." Her glance wandered to the crowds of passengers around them on the pier. "There are really some charming people aboard."

"I'm glad to hear it," he replied in a tone that meant nothing of the kind. "We'll have to compare notes in the Shetlands."

She let her eyes rest on him defiantly. "That's right. With Janice along, you don't know what to expect. Or do you?"

"Only time will tell. In the meantime, I'd suggest you forgo any invitations out on deck after dinner. It might not be as romantic but I'd prefer that you arrived in one piece. After all, I have a considerable sum invested in you already."

Her eyes flashed angrily. "You make it sound as if I'm bought and paid for. Are you telling me that—"

"I'm telling you to stop acting like an idiot and concentrate on keeping your head attached to your neck," he ordered, interrupting her ruthlessly. "I should think you'd be grateful for the advice."

After that, he lingered only long enough to retrieve her flowers from the dock where she'd dropped them and shove them in her arms before striding back to his taxi.

The door slammed and a moment later the car headed back toward the end of the pier, disappearing from sight into the traffic.

⋙ 5 ⋘

Afterward, Barbara couldn't even remember trudging back to her stateroom. She did recall her amazement that everything seemed to be much as usual when she was finally able to focus on the scene around her. That was surprising—everyone should have known that something cataclysmic had just occurred. Otherwise why should her knees feel as limp as spaghetti while her pulse was reacting like a seismograph during a volcanic eruption?

It was a relief to eventually close the door of her stateroom behind her and turn the key in the lock. Afterward, she threw the key on the dresser and tossed her purse beside it. She stared down at the bunches of freesias which she still clutched against her chest and felt tears flood her eyes. Shaking her head helplessly against the sudden misery, she went into the bathroom and filled the basin with cold water. She placed the flowers in it as a temporary measure. Later, she'd ask the steward for a vase but just then the thought of having to face anyone was too awful to contemplate.

All she wanted to do was sink onto her bed and close her eyes, hoping that the remembrance of that embrace on the pier would fade into oblivion. That way, she could continue to pretend that Kent Michaels didn't rate any importance in her life.

She sat down on the mattress and shoved her pillows into place before kicking off her shoes and curling up atop the spread. Just a few minutes peace, she decided, and then she'd go out on deck to the luncheon buffet. Just to show Kent, she'd find one of the nice-looking men she'd been carefully avoiding so far and change her tactics. That way, when the ship reached the Shetland Islands, she could trip down the gangway alongside a polite, attentive stranger and show Kent that his momentary aberrations didn't have any lasting effect on her, either.

She moaned softly at that flagrant lie and pushed up on an elbow to punch a more accommodating hole in her pillow—wishing that she had Kent at the mercy of her fist instead. Which was ridiculous because what she really wanted at that moment was to have him stretched out close beside her on the bed, holding her tight. Even the thought of being in his arms again sent her imagination on the rampage and she closed her eyes so that her dreams would linger.

Her reaction to the hectic morning must have taken a greater toll than she realized, because it wasn't long before her dreams slipped into sound sleep, her pillowcase still damp from her stray tears.

A strange metallic rattling at the door brought her awake later. She yawned slowly and frowned, wondering at the pale sunlight which still outlined the drapes at the cabin porthole. Catching a glimpse of her wrinkled skirt, her frown deepened until the events of the morning came flooding back and she sat upright.

Another noise at the locked cabin door made her swing her feet toward the floor. She had just opened her mouth to call out, "Half a minute—I'm coming," when a feminine voice from the hallway forestalled her.

"What's the matter with you? Why are you stopping?" the woman asked in an angry undertone that penetrated the cabin door.

"Because I think I just heard that damned steward down the corridor," came a muttered male voice. "If he's starting his round, he'll be checking her cabin any minute now and I'd just as soon not be in it when he does. Unless you have a better idea."

"But she'll be coming back aboard any minute. The ship's due to sail within the hour."

The voice sounded low and angry, but it wasn't difficult to recognize Janice Carling's distinctive tones and the knowledge kept Barbara frozen on the side of the bed. That plus the fact that her landlady and her companion had thought they were entering a vacant cabin.

"Why don't you tell me something I don't

know." Sarcasm oozed from the male voice, but it, too, sounded slightly familiar. Enough so that Barbara chewed nervously on the edge of her lip. "In fact, the more I think about it," the man went on, "I'm not sure ransacking her cabin is such a good idea. There isn't much chance of a payoff."

"Then why did Kent drag her along in the first place?" There was sheer feminine venom in Janice's words. "He could have left her in London occupying dear old Sir Philip Byron's flat."

"Maybe you haven't taken a good look at her lately. When she was diving for the shrubbery this morning, I was able to appreciate some of her finer points."

"Don't be coarse," Janice flared back in an annoyed whisper. "There's too much at stake for such talk."

"You asked a question"—Barbara could almost see his shrug as he continued—"that's my answer."

"I'm not impressed," Janice replied. "And you're hardly in a position to criticize my plans—after that fiasco of yours this morning."

"What do you mean? The whole idea was just to issue a warning. To force Michaels' hand—and maybe throw him off base. And it did. Of course what we didn't know was that you'd lose track of him so that now we have to scramble around and try to put the pieces back in order."

"But there was no reason to think he wouldn't be at the plane," Janice protested.

"Keep your voice down," the man ordered.

"Nobody's around," she muttered, but followed his orders so that Barbara had to risk tiptoeing to the door so that she could hear better. "I still think we have the place to ourselves," Jan went on.

"That's the way I like it," he announced. "Damn it all!"

"What's the matter now?"

"That was a tray being put outside in the hallway. It *is* the steward doing his rounds. We'll have to get out of here for now."

"But what about Barbara?"

"After she comes back aboard, she'll be going down to dinner in an hour or so. That's the time to check her cabin and I'll have plenty of leeway," he said, satisfaction underlying his tone.

"Well, you certainly lined up the posh bit for yourself." There was no hiding the vitriol in the brunette's words then. "I end up chasing around airports and you take an overnight cruise."

"Use your head—you're supposed to be in Kent Michaels' pocket—not aboard ship."

"But I don't know where he is."

"Then I suggest you find him." Her companion spaced out the order in a frozen undertone. "Don't forget, that's what you're getting paid for. So far, it hasn't been worth the money."

"Well, you haven't done any better," Janice countered.

"I know it." Barbara could hear him sigh before he went on. "And if we don't intercept the figures in that report of Sir Philip's before tomorrow afternoon, it'll be too late to buy in."

"You won't do anything foolish?" Janice pleaded, her voice even more impassioned. "Darling—there are other ways to make money. We'll find something if this doesn't work out."

"Christ! Don't start that again. I'm not going to risk my neck if I don't have to. With any luck, Kent's precious Barbara will still be in working order when we get to the Shetlands—unless she walks in her cabin unannounced."

"Then you think she has the notes here on board?"

"In a few hours, I should know for sure. Meanwhile, I want you to find Michaels. Ask about the charters at the airport. Maybe he took off for the Shetlands that way. It's what you should have done instead of coming here."

"I thought I should check in with you . . ."

"All right—you've checked. Now, get back out there. See if he's still in town, caught an early flight, or doubled back to London."

"But why should he do that?"

"Orders from the lordly Philip, of course. Wherever he went, get after him. And this time, find a way to search his belongings or don't bother reporting back."

"Darling, you don't mean that—"

He cut into her anguished plea with a terse, "Don't put it to the test. Now, let's get out of here because that steward's working closer. I'll go first and be on the pier to have a taxi waiting for you."

Barbara heard a rustle of movement and then

a whispered, "Right . . . It's clear," as she stayed motionless on her side of the door. She lingered for a full minute longer, hardly daring to breathe and then gathered her strength to finally unlock the cabin door and peer out into the blessedly empty corridor. As she stood there, heart thumping madly, the steward moved into sight and gave her a wide smile. "Miss Stratton," he said, and then his smile faded as she remained immobile. "Is there anything wrong? Maybe you'd like some tea?"

Barbara started to shake her head and then thought better of it. "Tea would be nice, thanks. If you have time."

"Sure thing. I'll bring it straight away."

She nodded and ducked back into the cabin, feeling safer when she was behind the closed door again. It had suddenly occurred to her that she wouldn't be able to recognize the man Janice was talking to and, under those circumstances, it wasn't smart to be seen in the corridor just then. In a half hour, she could go through the charade of having just come back aboard, but for the present, she couldn't risk letting him know that she'd overheard his conversation.

She sank on the edge of her bed again and dropped her head in her palms as she tried to think. The prospect of the evening ahead made her shudder, yet she couldn't go to the Purser's Office and complain that an unnamed and un-known fellow passenger might ransack her cabin during the night. At that rate, she'd probably be escorted from the ship before it sailed—right into a padded van at the end of the gangway.

"Damn!" she muttered in frustration and got up to stare through the porthole onto the pier below. Her gaze went from the milling passengers who were coming back aboard to the other side of the pier where the ship from Newcastle had docked. Movement on its bridge and along the promenade deck made her frown thoughtfully. Apparently it, too, was sailing shortly—otherwise there wouldn't be so much activity.

A knock on her cabin door made her jump and she went over to ask, "What is it?" before turning the key.

"I've brought your tea, Miss Stratton," came the steward's familiar voice.

"Sorry, I'd forgotten," Barbara said, as she unlocked the door and motioned for him to put the tray on the dresser. "Tell me," she went on when he'd straightened, "do you know anything about that ship on the other side of the pier?"

"Sure thing. Johannson Line. Goes overnight to Newcastle. A buddy of mine is a steward aboard."

"When does it sail?" she asked casually.

"Later today. It's just starting the run for this season. Calls in here three times a week for the next few months. If you'd like to look her over, they'll probably let you go aboard. It's not up to this ship, but not bad." His grin flashed. "When you're finished with your tray, just put it out in the hall and I'll collect it."

He was gone out the door before Barbara could

do more than nod her thanks. She stared at the tea tray afterward—finally pouring herself a cup and then with it still half-full, she picked up the telephone receiver to dial the Purser's Office. Maybe the idea that she had in mind wasn't feasible, but by then she was down to desperate measures.

Three hours later, she was peering out another porthole watching the homes of Bergen disappear to the stern, scarcely able to believe that she'd accomplished the seemingly impossible. She glanced around her at the austere cabin she'd been allotted on the Newcastle car ferry and drew a deep breath of relief. Until that moment, she'd been reluctant to acknowledge she'd managed to transfer ships without discovery.

The purser aboard the cruise ship had been suitably concerned when she'd reported a family crisis made it necessary for her to return to London. She had to talk a little faster when she vetoed his offer to make a reservation for her on the next flight to England. "I have an ear condition," she'd told him, searching for a plausible excuse, "and I'm really not supposed to fly." She couldn't very well say that the last place she wanted to be was the Bergen airport where Janice Carling would be looking over her shoulder before she could reach the check-in counter. Aloud, she said, "Is there any chance of passage on the ferry leaving for Newcastle? I could catch a train down to London tomorrow morning after they dock."

The purser had promised to do his best, calling

back ten minutes later to say there was space available. After that, it had been easy. She tipped her steward and arranged for him to take her bags to the other ship, adding a hefty tip to keep quiet about it. "Actually, I'm meeting someone— and I'd rather everyone didn't know," she told him. From the way his eyes lighted up, she knew that he suspected the worst, but the extra money would keep the story on the crew deck. By the time Janice's boyfriend discovered that she'd left the ship, it wouldn't matter.

Barbara reflected that her newfound talent for lying was amazing. Probably, she told herself darkly, it was because she'd been around Kent and picked up all the necessary pointers from him.

Even letting her mind wander that much was a mistake. Tears flooded her eyes at the realization of how alone and vulnerable she was without him. If only she'd thought to ask his plans—whether dodging Jan was deliberate or whether some emergency had arisen to keep him from the flight.

It would have been nice if he'd trusted her enough to mention those missing notes of Sir Philip's. But did he even know where they were? Animal, vegetable, or mineral—the old challenge came to mind. "Smaller than a bread box," she murmured and cast a frowning glance at her luggage, feeling more confused than ever.

That was the trouble with being a modern woman, she told herself bitterly. She was supposed to meet life's problems head on and glory in the confrontation. Instead, all she could think about were her bruised emotions after that farewell scene on the dock with Kent. It wasn't surprising that she'd taken the easiest way out rather than staying aboard the cruise ship and risking another confrontation—this time with an unknown adversary.

Now she would have to go back to the flat and try to get word to Kent through his stepfather. Somewhere on those premises, Sir Philip's telephone number should be listed. After that, she'd check into an inexpensive hotel and go back to playing tourist again. Naturally, if Kent wanted to come and see her, she'd try to fit him into her schedule.

Barbara's stomach tightened at that rationalization and she went over to sit on the edge of the bunk in her small cabin. Fit him in indeed! That was the trouble with out-and-out lies—she'd almost started to believe them herself.

At that moment, the framed schedule of meals atop the dressing table in the cabin fell noisily onto the floor. Barbara frowned as she stared down at it and then she realized that her inner qualms weren't due entirely to her miserable love life; the car ferry was starting to heave up and down in a disconcerting way as they went from the channel into the waters of the North Sea. A sudden spray of water against the glass of her porthole confirmed her suspicion that it was going to be a rough crossing indeed.

Turning green would be the final glorious touch

to the day, she told herself as she hastily opened her small bag and rummaged to see if she'd brought her motion sickness pills along. Fortunately, she found them on the first try and swallowed two with water before going out into the fresh air, hoping that they'd take effect and last until she sighted land again.

⇜ 6 ⇝

It wasn't until her taxi drew up in front of the flat in London at midafternoon of the next day that Barbara remembered Kent's warning about the building's roof repairs. After paying the driver, she stood on the curb and cast an anxious glance upward—reassured that there wasn't any scaffolding or a gaping hole on the front of the building, at least.

"Afternoon, miss. Need some help with your luggage?"

She brought her glance hastily down again to encounter the doorman from the restaurant nearby. "Thank you. I'd appreciate it," she told him as he picked up her bags. "I was just checking to make sure the roofers had finished. They have, haven't they?"

The doorman paused halfway up her stairs. "Roofers? Here on this block?"

She hesitated, key in hand, to stare back at

him. "Yes, of course. The ones working on this building."

"Haven't seen them, miss. 'Course I don't come on until eleven most mornings."

Relief flooded over her at that logical explanation and she smiled as she opened the door, holding it so he could bring her belongings inside. "That must be the reason. Thank you very much for your help," she went on as he straightened. "I feel as if I've been carrying those bags forever."

He lingered on the threshold. "My pleasure, miss. And I'll ask around about the roofers. Somebody on the block is sure to know."

As the door closed behind him, she went over to punch the lift button. When it arrived, she wedged the gate open with her hip while she transferred the bags to the tiny cubicle.

When the lift ground to its familiar shuddering stop a minute later, she managed the transfer process all over again. By concentrating on her bags she was able to postpone the possibilities of what she'd find behind the front door of the flat. She ignored her queasy stomach, telling herself that it was simply the aftermath of her skirmish with the North Sea the night before. And the less time she spent thinking about that the better! At least she'd managed to avoid being actually sick, although it was a close contest and necessitated spending more hours than she'd planned out on the open deck. By the time she had things under control and could safely lie down in her cabin, there'd been very little of the night left.

When she combined that with the local train she'd caught from Newcastle after the ship docked, it was small wonder that she'd looked like a pale wraith who'd walked all the way from Norway. Probably that was what had spurred the doorman to offer his help, she told herself as she moved her bags in tandem over to the flat door. He'd taken one look and decided that if he didn't lend a hand, she would have collapsed in front of his restaurant steps and upset his customers.

As she reached slowly in her purse for the flat key, her attention focused on the wooden door in front of her. Then her backbone stiffened; it was all very well to have retreated from Bergen, but she certainly wasn't going to be run out of a perfectly good Mayfair flat by an opportunistic, money-grubbing rental agent and her boyfriend. If they came calling in London, she'd be ready for them!

And if Kent came calling—mentally she threw up her hands in surrender at that prospect—and opened the door of the flat.

As she stepped over the threshold and stared into the neat, vacant rooms, she frowned in surprise. She'd expected tarpaper remnants or cracked pieces of plaster or grimy footprints; at least some reminder that the roofers had been on the scene.

She moved her bags in from the hall, but carefully left the door open until she'd gone through the flat, checking inside the big armoire and even looking behind the door in the bathroom. Only when she was satisfied that she was the sole occupant did she lock the door and put on the chain.

She left her purse on the marble shelf in the tiny foyer and went over to check the sloping ceiling in the living room. It appeared exactly as before and she knew immediately that the doorman downstairs would have a hard time locating a team of nonexistent roofers.

Which meant that Kent had deceived her one more time and she'd fallen for it like the idiot she was! For two cents, she'd not bother calling Sir Philip to report his missing stepson. Then she rubbed her forehead and attempted to think rationally. There was no use trying to convince herself that she didn't want to learn where Kent was. If Sir Philip didn't know of Kent's predicament he'd surely send some of his British colleagues searching for him.

First off, she'd have to be practical and try to locate Sir Philip. She detoured by the kitchen long enough to plug in the electric kettle for a cup of tea and then went over to peruse the London telephone directory with the letter "B." She hadn't really hoped for anything that easy and by the time the kettle whistled, she knew that Sir Philip Byron wasn't listed.

It didn't take long to pour the boiling water over a teabag and she looked around the kitchen thoughtfully, holding the steaming cup in her hand. There wasn't any bulletin board for listing addresses there. She arrived at the same conclusion after she'd gone through the dressing room. That left the tiny living room, but even a thorough check of the small directory by the phone didn't turn up more than the penciled numbers of a delicatessen and a nearby cleaners. She was sure of that because she called each one to confirm it.

The steam from her cup of tea made her eyes water and she reached in her purse to find a handkerchief. She pawed through the big shoulder bag and uttered a triumphant, "Finally!" when she discovered it underneath her passport case.

Then she froze as her fingers touched a small leather-covered book which had been pushed behind the pamphlet on Norwegian fjords. Kent's caption book! After she'd offered to keep it for him, she'd forgotten all about it.

She pulled the book from her purse and surveyed it thoughtfully. It was ridiculous not to open it, she told herself. After all, picture captions were hardly classified material.

One quick look inside was all she needed to forget her reluctance, because she'd happened on the lucky draw. Kent may have used the book for captions, but the very first page also listed five or six penciled telephone numbers.

Her glance slid over two American numbers at the top of the list with the area codes plus Texas addresses. Next was the number of the flat and still another with the initials J. C. after it.

"My dear landlady," Barbara murmured, but took time to check the London directory and confirmed that she was right. Then, finally, she smiled in triumph at the last two listings where P. B. was in the margin. But which was the right one? She frowned at the first telephone code and then consulted the London directory again, turning impatiently to a listing of rates for other cities in the U.K. When she managed to identify it as an Ascot number, she felt as if she could give Charlie Chan a run for his money. Evidently Sir Philip's home ground was Ascot when he wasn't staying in London. Now all that remained was the last number on Kent's list. "In for a penny— in for a pound," Barbara muttered and crossed her fingers after she'd carefully dialed.

There were only two rings before a clipped feminine voice came on the line. "Ministry," she said and waited expectantly.

"I beg your pardon?" Barbara replied when the silence lengthened. "Who is this, please?"

"What number are you ringing?" By then, the voice took on the quality of officialdom and Barbara knew she didn't have long before the receiver would bang down.

"I'd like to speak to Sir Philip Byron, please. It's important."

There was another pause before the secretary turned the tables efficiently. "Who is calling, please?"

"Barbara Stratton. And Sir Philip doesn't know me—but Kent—I mean—his stepson does."

"And you're calling from . . ."

"The flat," Barbara supplied obediently in the pause. "Sir Philip's *pied-à-terre* in Mayfair. Actually I'm his tenant—although I guess he doesn't know that either."

"In that case, Miss Stratton, perhaps you'll hang up and let me ring you back."

There was the sound of the receiver being replaced and afterward a buzzing noise which showed she'd been cut off.

Barbara frowned down at the receiver in her hand and then replaced it on the stand none too gently. "So much for British diplomacy." She reached for her cooling tea and took an angry swallow. "I should have gone to Hawaii in the first place," she told the picture of a bewhiskered yachtsman on the living room wall.

Before she could confide in him further, the phone rang sharply and she spilled tea down the side of the cup in her hurry to reach for the receiver again. "Hullo," she replied and then wondered what else she should say.

"Miss Stratton?"

It was a dignified deep male voice with BBC overtones this time, and Barbara sat up straighter on the couch. "Yes—I mean—this is Barbara Stratton," she finally got out.

"I'm sorry to have kept you waiting, but my secretary wanted to verify your call. That's one of the worst things about working in government—all this red tape which is so firmly wrapped around us. Incidentally, my stepson's been going 'round the bend trying to catch up with you ever since you left Bergen."

"Then you know where Kent is?" Relief poured over Barbara at the news and she didn't even try to hide it from Sir Philip.

"I didn't know he was misplaced." There was an undertone of laughter in his tone. "I thought *you* were the missing link. Actually"—in his British pronunciation the word came in two syllables instead of the usual three—"I shouldn't be leading you on. We've both been dreadfully concerned for your safety. You *are* all right, aren't you?"

Barbara's first impulse was to say, "Great, just great. There's nothing like a storm in the North Sea to set you up for the day." Fortunately, her early training came to the fore and she managed to say through clenched teeth, "I'm still functioning, thank you."

"Splendid." If he heard any tinge of sarcasm, Sir Philip chose to ignore it. "And you're all alone at the flat?"

"There may be some roofers still lurking around, but other than that . . ."

"Roofers?" Plainly it was a new subject to Sir Philip. "I don't quite understand."

"I'm sure that Kent can explain it to you." Barbara decided that she might as well quit while she was ahead, adding hastily, "If you do see him, you can tell him that I still have his caption book."

"I say—would you repeat that?" There was

no disguising the sudden interest in the older man's voice.

"I discovered a few minutes ago that I'm still carrying his caption book around with me. Perhaps you could ask him what I should do with it—I'd rather not leave it here at the flat."

"Certainly not."

That time, Sir Philip's reply held tinges of George III when he was giving orders to the Boston colonists, and Barbara reacted accordingly. "In that case, he'll just have to make arrangements to pick it up when it's convenient for both of us."

"Will you be at the flat long?"

"Not really," Barbara replied, making up her mind in a hurry. In her current state, she wasn't up to skirmishing with Kent. Besides, waiting around tamely smacked too much of being a convenience item—picked up and delivered whenever Sir Philip and his stepson fitted her in. "Actually," she said, taking a perverse delight in mimicking his pronunciation of the word, "I'm going out right away."

"Where?"

Her eyes widened at that stark query and she stared wildly around the room, trying to think of a plausible place she might be spending the rest of the afternoon. As her glance lit on a "This Week in London" brochure, she found her answer. "The flower show. The one at Chelsea. I'm just on my way."

If she hadn't known better, she could have

sworn that Sir Philip let out a groan, but he rallied quickly. "Perhaps we could meet you there and pick up the book."

"We?"

"I meant Kent, of course."

"I see. Then he's in London?" She tried to keep her query innocuous, as if she didn't really care one way or the other.

"Oh, yes. He's quite available. We both flew in a few hours ago." The older man sounded preoccupied as he handed out that snippet of information and went on without pause. "Do you know the grounds there at Chelsea?"

"Not too well," Barbara said, crossing her fingers as she spoke. If she'd told the truth, she would have had to admit that all she'd heard of Chelsea was that it was in the neighborhood of Sloane Square. Beyond that, she knew nothing about attending the famed flower show. "I'm sure that won't matter, though. Where would you like me to be?"

There was a smothered mutter—something about babes in the wood, she thought, before deciding that her imagination was playing tricks. Probably Sir Philip was simply clearing his throat. "There is a bandstand," he said after a considerable pause. "My secretary tells me that there's to be a concert there later this afternoon. It shouldn't be difficult for you to find."

After what she'd been through in the previous twenty-four hours, finding a bandstand sounded unbelievably simple. "What time should I be there?" she asked briskly.

"Probably an hour from now is as close as we can risk it," Sir Philip replied. "Considering the crowds and all."

"Whatever you say." She couldn't resist one last thrust. "Do we synchronize our watches?"

There was a well-bred chuckle. "That's what I like about you Americans," he told her, "your sense of humor. Unfortunately, trying for a split-second operation at the Chelsea Flower Show would make James Bond turn gray. It's been nice having this chat with you, Miss Stratton, but now I'd suggest you get a taxi straight away."

His receiver was replaced before Barbara could reply and she looked thoughtful as she replaced her own. There was an undercurrent of gentle warning in his last instructions that made her nerve endings quiver.

If she followed the schedule he'd suggested, there wasn't a spare minute for changing her clothes. The camel's hair suit she'd worn on the train with her dark-brown pullover sweater would have to do for the flower show, as well. At least her gold bowknot pin on the lapel and her chunky matching earrings added a little pizzazz, she decided, after checking her appearance at the hall mirror.

As she waited for the elevator to arrive, she thought back over her conversation with Sir Philip. It was strange that he hadn't said where Kent was—just that he was "available." Which meant he must be nearby or he couldn't make the meeting in Chelsea.

By the time she reached the street, some hurried footsteps made her start nervously until she found that they belonged to her new acquaintance, the restaurant doorman.

"Just wanted to say that I've checked the boys on the street and—"

She cut in before he could finish, ". . . nobody knows anything about any roofers. Right?"

"Blimey, that's it. I figured you must have made a mistake on the dates. Too bad you weren't betting on somebody fixing the pipes—that way, you could have collected."

"Next time I'll know better," she told him solemnly, taking the easy way out. "In the meantime, could you possibly find a taxi for me?"

He beamed. "S'pleasure, miss. I'll go up to the corner. There should be one cruising Jermyn Street. Half a mo."

It wasn't long until he was back, beckoning triumphantly toward the cab just behind him. "Where to, luv?" he asked, opening the door with a flourish when it pulled alongside.

Barb smothered her amusement at the way their acquaintance had progressed. "The Chelsea Flower Show, please," she said, pressing a pound note into his willing palm.

"Righto, m'dear." He ushered her into the cab and slammed the door before giving the address to the driver.

It only took a few blocks of bumper-to-bumper traffic before Barb realized why Sir Philip had given her so much time to reach Sloane Square.

Her driver had evidently flipped a mental coin

and decided that going through Knightsbridge
was the best route, but it turned out that the
elegant shopping district was just as crowded as
Piccadilly. At least it provided interesting display
windows while they waited for lights at the various
intersections. There was especially thick traffic
as they neared Harrods, the huge department
store with its famous food halls and unique private
zoo.

Once her cab turned left along Sloane Street,
the traffic thinned for a few blocks when they
left the retail shops behind and the buildings became expensive flats with an occasional embassy
to add special dignity to the neighborhood.

The sidewalks were still crowded, only by now
there were uniformed school children mingling
with the shoppers and other residents who were
headed for the small parks with restful shade trees
and velvety lawns which could be seen nearby.

Barbara stared through the cab window as if
she'd never viewed any of the sights before. It
was a deliberate tactic because if she'd relaxed
for a moment and tried to anticipate what was
going to happen when she met Kent again, she'd
never get through the entrance of the flower show.
The best thing was to concentrate on her surroundings, breathe deeply to subdue her bounding
pulse, and try to pretend that this wasn't going
to be the most important afternoon in her life.

She unzipped her purse to make sure that
Kent's caption book was still nestled inside and
then just as carefully zipped her bag closed again.

Since it had turned out to be a logical and splendid excuse for the projected rendezvous, she had no intention of making a mistake there.

She swayed on the seat as the cab slowed after reaching busy Sloane Square with its popular stores and eating places—finally making a right turn onto another crowded street.

The cab driver must have seen her anxiously checking her watch because he shoved aside the glass partition to say, "Sorry it's such a slow trip, miss. Sloane Square's always a bottleneck and with the flower show in Chelsea . . ." He shrugged his shoulders as the cab inched forward again.

"I didn't realize it would be this crowded," Barb said, peering out at the thronged sidewalks.

"We should get a break soon when I turn off this street. Traffic control's pretty strict about keeping things moving around the show entrance. Has to be with thousands of people."

"Thousands?" she said faintly.

"Lord, yes. Haven't you been watching the telly? They set a new attendance record on opening day." His eyes met hers momentarily in the rearview mirror. "Pity you can't go for a preview like the royals. No standing in a queue then."

She chewed nervously on her thumbnail. "Are the lines—er—the queues—apt to be long?"

"That depends—you'll find out soon," he replied, speeding up appreciably as they finally turned into a residential street with apartment houses on either side.

There was a parklike enclosure with some older

buildings which could be seen at the end of the street. "Soldiers' home," the driver volunteered and pointed toward a crowded entrance. "That's the flower show gate."

"You mean all of those people are planning to go through it?" Barbara gasped in disbelief. "How big are the grounds, for heaven's sake?"

"Twenty-three acres," the driver responded proudly. "That's how they can accommodate 250,000 people during a four-day run. Actually this is the Chelsea Royal Hospital—the garden blokes just transform the grounds for the occasion."

As the cab drew closer, Barbara could see the tops of huge tents erected side by side, making the show look like a tremendous circus. The sound of a band playing somewhere near and flags flying in the breeze added to the festive atmosphere.

"This has been going on here since 1913," the driver confided proudly when the cab slowed to a crawl as they neared the entrance. "Even before that the Royal Horticulture Society was in the news. Queen Victoria made them a big present of money because that husband of hers liked to garden. Nobody's looked back since." He braked at the curb, turning to say, "This is as close as I'll be able to stop. You'll make better time walking from here anyway."

"Yes, of course." Barbara fumbled in her purse for some money, taking care to add a generous tip. "I hope that somebody can give me directions when I get inside."

He nodded reassuringly. "Just ask anybody who's wearing a uniform. And from what I can see, there are plenty of them around."

As Barbara got out on the sidewalk and started toward the entrance, his meaning became clear. There was a solid phalanx of policemen and women paying close attention as patrons surged through the gate. For an instant, Barbara hesitated, wondering if she'd happened into a bomb scare and then as she saw the unperturbed expressions on the people buying tickets, she decided that she was letting her imagination run riot unnecessarily.

There wasn't time to ask questions from the busy ticket sellers, but she did manage to line up behind a kind-looking old gentleman who was waiting to get in. "Could you tell me what's happening?" she asked him as they shuffled along. "Why are all the police at the entrance?"

"Happens all the time now, love," he told her. He shook his shaggy gray head as if modern happenings were beyond belief. "We either get letter bombs or a terrorist bunch is killing innocent people. You never know what's going to happen next. In the old days at Chelsea, nobody had to worry about some lunatics blowing up the pelargoniums. A bloody shame, that's what it is."

Barbara could only nod her agreement before they were going through the entrance. When a policewoman politely asked her to open her purse and then waved her through after searching the contents, it was a sobering experience. Enough that she forgot to ask about the location of the bandstand which had been foremost in her mind.

She was propelled along in the mob of friendly people headed for a big circus tent ahead of her. Sudden curiosity made her decide that she could sneak a look inside and still be on time for her appointment at the bandstand.

As she approached the tent, booths on either side of the cement walkway featured garden furniture, gazebos, horticultural magazines, and even garden gift shops with trowels and shovels bearing bright red bows. Each shop seemed to have its quota of customers with more waiting to spend their money.

By then, she'd reached the big canvas enclosure and drew an astonished breath as she went inside. It *was* like a circus, she decided, only instead of three main rings there were three or four main aisles dividing the length of the huge enclosure. Each aisle contained a mass of humanity, intent on savoring the fabulous floral displays.

Directly in front of her was a rose exhibit with almost every inch covered either by floribundas, hybrid teas, or climbers on trellises. The bushes were in full bloom, cleverly "planted" in real turf brought in for the occasion. In addition, there were bouquets of other prize varieties of every color. The salespeople were doing a brisk business, but if customers couldn't make up their minds, they could buy catalogs for ordering at home.

While Barbara was still savoring the rose fragrances, she discovered that the next display featured an equally impressive collection of dahlias with blooms of every size and color. "How on earth do you get dahlias to bloom at this time of year?" she asked a smiling attendant.

"They're all forced just for this show," she was told. "You'll find every variety of flower here at Chelsea. Every one's in full bloom and at the peak of condition. That's why this is the world's largest horticultural event—and, we think, the very best. If you prefer to buy seeds"—she gestured across the aisle to another display where packets were selling rapidly—"you can have those, too."

"Something for everybody," Barbara murmured.

"Exactly. Even down to champagne and lobster when you get hungry."

Barbara stared at the woman. "Are you serious?"

"Very much so. Mind you, it's a bit dear, but well worth it. You can't miss the spot where they serve it—close to the bandstand. Just follow the sound of the music."

"The bandstand?" Barbara looked guiltily at her watch and decided she'd better not linger any longer. "Which way is it, please?"

The woman frowned, seeing her anxious expression. "You'd best go out the back of the tent," she said, gesturing in that direction. "Turn left and look for the signs on the walkway. It isn't far."

Barbara started for the back of the tent as she'd been directed and then, catching sight of a sleek dark head at the end of the aisle, paused for a moment in confusion. Surely Janice Carling hadn't deserted Bergen just to see the Chelsea Flower Show. As she stared blindly at the exhibit in front of her, Barbara tried to juggle the possibilities of such a happening. Since Kent was back in town, too, it was quite possible that the two of them had eventually gotten together in Norway and returned to England on the same flight. That being the case, it wasn't strange that Janice had come to the flower show with him—before they went on to a more exciting destination. The possibility made Barbara's lips come together in a bleak line and prompted a saleswoman in charge of a nearby booth to say, "Feeling peaky, dear? That's not surprising with all these people. I'd invite you to sit down but"—she gestured toward her small display stall which was crowded with white plastic strawberry barrels—"I don't even have a chair."

"Thanks very much, but it isn't necessary," Barbara reassured her hastily. "I was just woozy for a moment."

"Are you sure?"

"Very sure," Barbara told her, trying to edge away from the helpful woman who bore a striking resemblance to Miss Marple. Then she glanced around and decided a great many women in the tent looked almost the same. Obviously her imagination was running rampant, she thought, or most of them bought their sweaters and skirts at the same Marks & Spencer store.

"Well, if you're not," the woman called after her, "there's an aid station bang on to the statuary display outside. Just look for the cupids and the goddesses—you can't miss all those naked bodies."

Even with the throngs of people around her, the woman's distinct British tones cut through the air like a laser beam. Heads turned as the flower show patrons stared to see who was headed for the naked bodies and, for a moment, Barbara's flushed face attracted more attention than the prize-winning orchid display at the end of the aisle.

She forgot all about the possibility of running into Janice Carling as she bolted for the exit and pulled up outside, relieved to be beyond the curious eyes.

"Right by the naked bodies as advertised," came a mocking masculine voice behind her. "What won't you Americans be hunting for next?"

She whirled and then shook with helpless laughter as she leaned against a piece of statuary. "Derek," she got out finally. "Whatever are you doing here?"

"Well, I'm not buying that nymph or whatever it is that's supporting you at the moment," the antique dealer told her as his amused glance swept over the statuary.

"I can't see why you don't approve," she said.

"That Grecian urn he's carrying keeps him respectable—for a nymph, that is. Maybe he's what my garden needs."

Derek started to chuckle. "By the time you paid the freight on him all the way across the Atlantic, you'd be skint for sure. If it's just naked bodies you're after, I have some paintings in my Knightsbridge shop that are a much better value."

"The way my checkbook looks at the moment, I couldn't buy much more than a postcard—let alone old masterpieces." She kept her voice light as she surveyed his relaxed figure in slacks and sport coat. "Is this a day off for you?"

"What makes you say that?"

"Well, I haven't seen any antique shops since I've been here, although I think that's the only thing that's missing." She managed a quick look at her watch and grimaced. "Oh, Lord—I have to dash. I'm late now. Maybe we can get together later in the week."

"Wait a minute." He caught her arm when she started to turn away. "You can't do a disappearing act on me. Not when it's been such a stroke of luck meeting here in the first place."

Barbara tried not to sound as frantic as she was feeling by then. "Really, I'd like to stay—but I *am* meeting someone."

"Well, I can walk along with you. Actually, I've seen about all I can take of this 'green thumb' bit. I was on my way to have a drink of something and wash down all my newfound knowledge," he said, falling into step beside her as they started down a crowded path between two display tents.

"Then I won't be taking you out of your way," she said in some relief. "I guess the champagne and lobster bar is close by the bandstand."

"Couldn't be closer," he said with a tone of pleased discovery. "The concert is the floor show for all of us who like a bit of the bubbly. I say, what about combining forces?"

"Really, I don't think that's a good idea this time—" she began, only to have him cut in.

"We could give it a go—probably your chap wouldn't mind sharing a drink. You can tell him that I'm a family friend."

Barbara started to say that she already had and then thought better of it. Instead, she stalled a little longer, asking, "What makes you think that I'm meeting a man?"

"That's easy." Derek put out a hand to protect her from a toddler who was carrying an ice cream bar at arm's length as they turned onto another crowded pathway. "You wouldn't be worried about being late if it were another woman."

"That's not a very nice thing to say."

"Strike me down if it's not the truth." He held up his palm as if taking an oath and pulled a long face. "That's safe around here—there isn't room to fall down. Not in this scrum."

Barbara wasn't sure what a scrum was, but she did realize that the sound of band music was getting louder. That should mean they were nearing the bandstand with Kent on the lookout for her.

Surely it would be easier to let him ease Derek on his way than to make a fuss. The possibility that Kent might simply collect his caption book and wave a farewell wasn't worth thinking about.

Her subconscious surfaced long enough at that point to argue that if such a miserable thing happened, having Derek by her side might at least help her save face.

"I say, you're looking awfully pale today," Derek said with an intense glance. "What's been going on in your life? I thought that cruises were supposed to work a transformation."

"How did you know . . . ," she began.

". . . that you were on a cruise? An educated guess. Americans like a bit of luxury when they're traveling. Besides, that man who answered the phone at your flat mentioned you were leaving for Norway. I had no idea that you'd be back so soon."

"I didn't stay for the whole cruise," she retorted, without explaining further. Just then, making small talk was proving an effort and she was wishing that she'd chosen someplace—anyplace—without the mobs of people that the Chelsea Flower Show had attracted.

"I see." Derek must have taken the hint because he didn't probe further. Instead, he flashed a crooked smile and said, "What you need is some champagne therapy. It's guaranteed to fight dandruff, bring color to your cheeks, and cure insomnia."

It was impossible to ignore his good-natured

teasing and Barbara smiled despite herself. "None of those is a problem right now."

"Then we'll sit down at a convenient table and you can tell me exactly what your problem is," he said, steering her toward a shaded restaurant area when they reached the end of the path. "When I'm not searching the suburbs for Hepplewhite and Chippendale, I hand out free advice. But only on Tuesday and Thursday afternoons. Fortunately, you've picked the right day."

"Derek, be serious." She pulled to a stop at the side of the walkway and looked around her. If she hadn't known that she was in modern-day London, she could have expected to see Queen Victoria and her entourage visiting the bandstand which sat in the middle of a big green lawn directly ahead of them. The members of the military musical group providing the concert wore bright red uniforms with enough gold braid to supply an entire Gilbert and Sullivan repertory company. Their conductor was a lean and dignified officer who wore his cap square atop his head and used his baton to slash through the afternoon air with geometric precision.

His audience sat spellbound, thoroughly enjoying the free concert as they sat on the grass, sprawled against trees or, for a fortunate few, occupied folding wooden chairs.

Derek must have been watching her closely, because he asked, "Why are you looking like that? As if you'd never seen a band concert before?"

She gave him an apologetic smile as she tried to explain. "This country is so full of contrasts. You go from punk rock concerts in Edinburgh to brass bands in Chelsea. I have a hard time keeping up."

"We're not any different from the rest of the world. Perhaps a bit more crowded together, that's all. 'Something for everybody'—that's my motto. Have you seen your chap yet?"

Barbara had been carefully searching the crowd around the bandstand, but she'd tried to be discreet about it and she felt a flush go over her cheeks at his question. "No. He must have been held up. Don't let me keep you, though. It's been great fun seeing you again . . ." Her voice trailed off when she saw that he wasn't paying the slightest attention to her attempt to send him on his way.

"See that empty table at the restaurant—right by that low hedge?" He was pointing toward a spot that adjoined the bandstand area.

"Yes, but—"

"No 'buts.' I insist that you share some champagne with me," he said, taking her arm to march her in that direction. "If you see your date, all you have to do is wave and he'll come running. Especially if you hold up a bottle of champagne in the other hand."

"Well, I suppose it couldn't hurt anything . . ."

"I've had more enthusiastic acceptances to my invitations, but I'll forgive you this time," he said, pulling out a chair at the table he'd indicated. "There now, you can see the whole bloody concert area so I insist that you relax."

"Thanks very much." She gave him a fleeting smile. "It's certainly a lot better than leaning against a tree trunk. And much more comfortable than sitting on the grass."

"Wait until you try it with champagne." He hovered by the table. "What would you like to go with it? Prawns, lobster—I think there's even some caviar."

"That's certainly more lavish than the strawberries and cream at Wimbledon," she said in surprise. "Are you serious?"

"Of course. What do you fancy?"

She opted for the truth. "Would you believe me if I said a cup of tea?"

He cupped his ear and leaned forward. "Sorry, I didn't hear that."

She gave up then and leaned back in surrender. "All right. A glass of champagne—but only one. I haven't had much to eat today and it's murder on an empty stomach. It wouldn't improve your social standing if you had to carry me out."

"I'd be happy to risk it. No?" His expression lightened again. " 'Alf a mo' while I go place our order and then I'll be right back."

As soon as he'd disappeared toward the bar where patrons were thronged to give their orders of seafood and champagne, Barbara rose to her feet again. Standing by her chair, she scanned the grounds next to the bandstand, trying to identify Kent among the audience. It wasn't like him to be late to an appointment, she thought with a worried look and then sat down again. There wasn't anything she could do except wait until he appeared. Surely Sir Philip couldn't have meant another bandstand—

Derek was back with a waiter who carried a bottle of champagne in an ice bucket and two glasses. "You can put it right alongside," he instructed after the man had opened the frosty bottle and wrapped a napkin around it.

Barbara waited until the waiter was out of hearing before she reproved Derek, who was filling the stemmed glasses with bubbling, golden liquid. "This doesn't look like a small glass. Honestly, I'd be flat out on the table before we ever reached the bottom of that bottle."

"Who knows—we may have company." He raised his glass in a toast. "What shall we drink to? Old friends—new friends. I can't remember the rest of it."

"Happy days," she said, settling the question for him, and took a swallow of her wine. "Umm. That's nice."

Derek followed suit and a pleased smile came over his face. "There's something wonderfully decadent about drinking champagne at this time of day. Much more fun than slaving away at the shop."

"Or doing most anything," Barbara replied, her tone deliberately light. The low rays of the afternoon sun gave her an excuse for keeping her glance hooded and also provided a chance to survey the man across the table.

Derek chose to wear his hair longer than most of the people around them, but it seemed to fit in with his ascetic features and worldly air. When she'd first seen him, she'd thought he should occupy an absentminded professorial niche, but in the sunlight at Chelsea she wondered if he hadn't contrived to achieve that result. It wouldn't hurt his role as an expert in the antique trade and probably was especially effective with his women customers. Certainly he was amiability itself—or appeared to be. She did wonder how he'd react when he met opposition. When she'd even protested mildly a few minutes before, he'd overridden her objections with charming but efficient thoroughness.

Just then, he appeared content to bask in the sunshine and keep a watching brief on the throngs of people enjoying the concert. When the band struck up a spirited rendition of "Scotland the Brave," Barbara forced herself to sit back and relax, because it would have been an effort to shout over the music.

"No sign of your bloke yet?" Derek poured himself more champagne and topped her glass when the band had finally finished to enthusiastic applause.

"I'm afraid not." Barbara's lips tightened, as she glanced around her. She had tried to be so careful in her surveillance of the crowd and yet Derek hadn't missed a trick. For the first time, she felt a frisson of apprehension and she shivered.

"You're not cold, are you?"

He was only being courteous, Barbara thought and forced herself to meet his intent glance. "No, of course not. What do you say when that happens? Someone's walking over your grave?" And why on earth did she have to bring up *that* subject just then, she thought as soon as the words left her mouth.

A half-smile touched his thin lips and then was gone. "I don't think you've ever mentioned exactly who you're waiting for. Could it be the man who answered the phone at the flat that day?"

"As a matter of fact—yes." Barbara didn't see any reason to hide the truth. "His name's Kent Michaels. He's another American."

"A friend from home?"

"Not really." She started to smile as she realized that Kent had asked the same questions when he heard about Derek that first time.

"Perhaps I've said something to amuse you."

She glanced up then and encountered his intent gaze. Even as she shook her head she was thinking that his dispassionate glance was a giveaway. Derek *wasn't* amused and he wasn't just a carefree Britisher out for fun as he listened to a band concert. There was definitely something else on his mind.

It wasn't long in coming. "I wonder if you know this Kent Michaels as well as you think you do?"

"What on earth do you mean by that? After all, I'm meeting him for a band concert—not sneaking away for an illicit weekend at Brighton. Or is it Bournemouth where you go?"

He ignored that, saying stiffly, "I certainly didn't mean to upset you, but I thought that you might appreciate a little advice. After all, you are a long way from home and, as a friend of Aunt Margaret's . . ." He paused as she started to laugh.

"Is that all? I appreciate your concern, Derek, but really—" she managed to say finally, amused that all her worrying was for nothing. Apparently the antique dealer had decided that she needed a good chaperone and he'd taken over the job.

"It isn't necessary," he said, finishing her sentence for her.

"Well, I do think you have the wrong end of the stick," she began and then broke off again because Janice Carling in a bright yellow suit was approaching their table. "Good Lord!"

"Someone you know?" Derek asked, turning to follow her gaze.

"You could say so." Barbara summoned a smile to greet her. "Hi, Janice. Everybody in London must have come to Chelsea today."

"At least all the tourists," the brunette said. Her tone warmed appreciably as she surveyed Derek who was getting to his feet. "Are you a friend of Barbara's or do you just come with the table?"

"A bit of both," he began.

"Janice Carling—Derek Redmayne," Barbara said, deducing that her landlady's call wasn't going to be a fleeting one. Especially not with a presentable man and champagne on view. Aloud she said, "Can you join us?" Then before Janice could answer, she went on hopefully, "But maybe you're not alone."

"I am for the moment," Janice purred as Derek lost no time in pulling up a chair for her and beckoned for another glass.

"When did you get back to London?" Barbara asked after Janice took her first sip of champagne. "I'm surprised that you're not in the Shetlands."

"Everybody's surprised today," Janice replied somewhat bitterly. She took a deep swallow from her glass and directed an amused glance across the table at Derek. "Don't look so disapproving, Mr. Redmayne. I promise not to finish your bottle." Reaching over to pull it from the ice bucket, she surveyed the label with raised eyebrows. "Nothing but the best. You must be in a profitable line of business."

"I manage to keep the wolf from the door," Derek said, looking down his nose at her.

"Derek's in the antiques' business," Barbara contributed. "He has shops in Knightsbridge and Brighton."

"Do tell." Janice ran a finger down the stem of her glass and directed a meaningless smile in Barbara's direction. "Nice for you. Friends in every port—so to speak."

Barbara decided that she didn't have to be polite and endure any more sniping, no matter how insistent her companions were. She gathered up her bag and started to push back her chair. "I'm sorry to break this up, but I really have to go. I have an appointment . . ."

"With Kent," Janice murmured. "I know. He may be a little late."

"What do you know about it?" Derek asked, his tone sharp.

"Darling, don't be coarse," Janice reproved and then broke off at Barbara's swift, indrawn breath. A cynical look came over the brunette's features and she said, "What do you know! The innocent has finally tumbled."

"Janice, shut up," Derek ordered.

"No—I want to know," she insisted, keeping her glance on Barbara. "What gave our game away?"

"Those were the same words you used aboard the ship in Bergen. When the two of you were talking outside my cabin. I thought the man's voice sounded familiar even then." Barbara shook her head as if to clear it when she stared across the table at Derek, scarcely able to comprehend that the hard-eyed man was the person she'd found on her doorstep the week before.

"Exactly how much did you overhear?" he asked in an ominous undertone.

"Enough to decide a retreat was in order." Barbara worked to steady her voice. "I wasn't keen about meeting you in my cabin at midnight—especially when I didn't know what you were looking for."

"Spare us that," Janice said, her words crisp again. "I can't believe that Kent didn't let a few choice morsels drop. He certainly had plenty of time at the flat or squiring you around in Bergen."

"A fact which annoyed Janice considerably," Derek pointed out. From his lack of expression, he might have been commenting on the price of soybeans or New Zealand butter. "I told her that she was wasting her time with Michaels, but she didn't believe me."

"Darling, you know that isn't true," Janice protested. "I was simply following your orders. It isn't my fault that you botched the whole project."

"You shouldn't be so quick to condemn," Derek said, leaning forward to put his elbows on the table. "Otherwise Barbara wouldn't be straining at the leash now to meet her dear Kent. I trust that you were able to sidetrack him successfully this time." The last comment came as he momentarily glanced at Janice.

Her lips tightened—so did her fingers on her glass in front of her. "For the moment—if you don't drag this out too long."

"I like to think that my sense of timing is as good as the next man's." He went on to Barbara in the same conversational vein, "It's something I've had to develop in business. Otherwise, I would have been bankrupt in a year."

She sent a look of intense dislike across the table. "You can't expect me to stand up on a chair and cheer over your dirty dealings." Anger made it difficult to get her words out, as she added, "I can't believe that your family would approve— your Aunt Margaret certainly doesn't have the slightest idea that you're mixed up in such things."

Derek pushed his champagne glass back so violently that some of the contents spilled and ran onto the table. "Good God! As if I care what that dried-up woman knows! She thinks I should be happy to make a pound or two in a fortnight selling jet beads and Victorian sewing bits to the tourists. Mind you, she'd have a stroke if she realized that she'd helped my cause by recommending the flat to you. I thought of that maneuver when she wrote and said you were coming over here. A friend at court never hurts."

"Well, all it's done so far is drag us to this stinking flower show to drink warm champagne," Janice complained to him.

"Be thankful that obliging doorman told us where Barbara was headed—and that we were just a bit behind her taxi," Derek said, directing a scathing glance toward Janice. "We'd still be stumbling around St. James Square if I'd waited for you to do your job."

"At least I had sense enough to keep the flat under surveillance," she countered and then blotted her forehead with the back of her hand. "How much longer are we going to risk sitting around here?"

Derek shot her another annoyed glance, but he must have seen the logic in her comment, because he said, "Not long. Now, my dear Barbara, listen closely and do what I say. That way, you won't get hurt. Put both your hands on the table where I can see them."

"Why—why should I?" Barbara retorted angrily. She struggled to push her chair back when his next words stopped her.

"Because otherwise you won't leave these grounds in very good shape. I'm afraid I had to doctor your drink a little. By now, you'd never make it to the gate and if you raise a fuss"—he pointed a finger at her, as she opened her mouth to protest—"no one's going to listen."

At that moment, Barbara could believe him. Even before he'd spoken, her insides had been rumbling alarmingly, but she'd put that and her overwhelming weariness down to the fact that she'd drunk the champagne on an empty stomach and had so little sleep the night before. She tried valiantly to pull herself together, but the effort showed Derek's "doctoring" had delivered a lethal blow.

"Damn it all!" she moaned in disgust and rubbed her eyes, trying hard to fight the lethargy that was creeping over her.

"Just do as you're told and you'll live to complain to dear Aunt Margaret another day," Derek snapped again. "Janice—go through her purse. In your lap, stupid," he lashed out at the other woman when she took the bag from Barbara's weak grasp and put it on the table. "She must have those notes somewhere."

By that time, it was beyond Barbara's ability to stop them physically; indeed it required a tremendous effort to keep her head erect instead of letting it flop on the table in front of her. She did manage to upset her champagne glass in the desperate hope that a waiter would respond. Someone would have to believe her . . .

The man appeared at their table before she realized it, righting her glass and using a damp towel to tidy the surface.

When she licked her dry lips and tried to speak to him, Derek leaned forward, ostensibly to reassure her. His hand gripped her shoulder in warning as he said loudly, "My dear, it doesn't matter. We'll have the mess cleaned up in no time, but I think it best if you don't have any more to drink right now." The last came when the waiter lingered to refill her glass. Barbara sat helplessly, aware that Derek's broad wink at the man had convinced him she was just another silly woman who'd had too much to drink.

Derek waited until the waiter returned to his station before he sat back. "All right, get on with it," he ordered Janice, who delved into Barbara's purse again. "What have you found?"

"There's only one thing that looks possible," the woman replied, sounding uncertain as she pulled out Kent's caption book. "The rest is just the usual."

"Hand it over," Derek commanded, reaching across for it.

Even in her dazed state, Barbara knew that she couldn't let him have it. It was hard to focus her eyes as she looked around for help—just to discover that the neighboring patrons were engrossed in their own champagne celebrations and not paying the slightest attention to anything else. Only the waiter who'd cleared up the spilled wine bothered a glance in her direction, and he seemed to shake his head in disgust.

"Tha's mine," she said, trying to sound forceful as Janice passed the caption book in front of her.

Derek sent a taunting smile her way when he saw that she couldn't even make her hand reach out for it. "Relax, my dear. If it's yours, then you won't mind my taking a look," he said smoothly. "Why don't you just put your head down and take a nap."

"My God, what will people think . . ." Janice said fastidiously, her voice rising.

"Just what we want them to, of course. The little lady's gotten herself sloshed. That way, no one will pay any attention when her good friends carry her out a few minutes from now." He was rifling through the pages of the book as he spoke. "Damn! It's hard to make anything out from this except that it belongs to Kent. That's good enough for me, though. We'll take her back to your place, Janice," he said, shoving the book in his pocket and putting a steely hand at Barbara's elbow. "In an hour or so, she should be able to give us any answers we're still missing. It's clear that she's in this project up to her neck."

"M'not."

Derek bent to hear Barbara's mumbled comment, his eyes alive with malicious laughter.

"What's that, dear? Speak up—didn't anyone ever tell you to enunciate your words. An American failing, I fear."

"Derek, for God's sake! Stop playing cat and mouse. Let's get out of here," Janice urged.

All touches of humor drained from his face as he turned his attention to her. His glance was icy as he said through a tight jaw, "I've told you before not to give me orders. Maybe that ex-husband of yours had the right idea, after all. There's only one way to make any impression on that silly mind of yours."

"You wouldn't . . . you wouldn't dare," she said, quailing visibly under his blast. "I won't stand for any more of that—I've told you."

"You'd be far better off if you hadn't told me so many things," he advised her. "That's another fault of yours and quite unnecessary. You should know by now that I seldom forget anything of importance. Or anything that might come in handy in my . . . work." There was a pause before he uttered the last word—clearly meant as a warning.

They were so engrossed in their threats that Barbara decided to concentrate all her energy in trying to get help. She meant to beckon the waiter—the only person around who was even looking her way—but she barely managed to lift her hand an inch off the table before Derek caught the movement from the corner of his eye.

"Bloody hell!" he ground out, slapping her fingers down again. Then, deciding that he couldn't risk any more outbursts, he said, "You carry her purse, Jan. It's time to get her out of here. I'm not sure how long that tranquilizer lasts, but I'll keep her face against my shoulder. Now what do *you* want?"

The last came as the waiter materialized at his elbow again.

The gray-haired man said, "Your bill, sir," in a deferential tone, dropping it on the table as he reached over to extract the champagne bottle from the ice bucket. "I'm sure you'd like to finish this. Allow me."

"That isn't necessary," Derek said with barely suppressed violence, pulling out his wallet.

In her groggy state, Barbara wasn't sure what happened next—whether Derek bumped the waiter's arm or the man simply missed his aim. One thing was sure; instead of hitting the champagne glass at the edge of the table, the effervescent wine went straight into Derek's lap.

"You bloody idiot!" Derek howled, almost dancing in anger as he surged to his feet. "Look what you've done!"

"I *am* sorry, sir." The waiter looked at the bottle he was still holding and awkwardly put it back in the ice bucket. "Of course we'll take care of any inconvenience. Let me call the manager."

"That isn't necessary." Derek was scrubbing

at the front of his slacks with his handkerchief. "All I want is to get out of this place."

"What's happening here, Judkins?" Another gray-haired man in a dark suit with a managerial lapel pin came up beside them.

"I'm afraid that I've gotten this gentleman somewhat damp, sir," the waiter began, only to be interrupted by a uniformed policeman who sauntered around the hedge.

"You're causing a bit of a disturbance, you know," he said, surveying them thoughtfully. "Shall we sort things out in the office over there?"

"There's nothing to sort out—" Derek was almost apoplectic with rage by then. "My only object is to get away from these bumbling fools . . ."

"I'd prefer it if you'd keep your voice down, sir," the constable advised him firmly. "Are you the only one involved?"

He glanced at Janice, but she held out her palms helplessly, saying, "Don't look at me. I'm just sitting here—minding my own affairs."

"And you, miss?" The official glance rested momentarily on Barbara.

She tried. For the rest of her life, she would remember how she tried to say all the things that whirred through her dazed mind like a montage in a film scenario.

Then to her complete frustration and chagrin, she saw her surroundings gradually dissolve into a descending darkness. Under the eyes of all of the watching restaurant patrons and the nearest concert-goers who were torn between a choice of entertainment, Barbara's head fell forward. She closed her eyes as the table came up to meet her—dropping into oblivion with the fumes of expensive French champagne all about her.

7

At least it was cool, Barbara thought when she surfaced again. Whoever would think that champagne would turn out to be so practical. Even so, it was easier to keep her eyes closed because she couldn't face all those horrified faces—not until she'd gathered her strength.

The sound of music came dimly to her ears and she identified the "Skye Boat Song." It was a lilting rendition done with a tenor and violins. She smiled, thinking it really was an improvement over the rest of the band's program. An instant later, she realized that brass band concerts didn't feature violins or tenors, for that matter—and her eyes opened wide.

One glance around was enough to make her shut them again. She shook her head to clear it, but that was a mistake and she moaned as her eyelids flickered and she sat up. "Oh, Lord— I feel awful," she managed to say.

"Well, at least you've decided to rejoin the world."

It was Kent's voice and she stared across the living room of the flat, attempting to focus on him where he stood on the threshold. There seemed to be other people, too, and the strange part was that they all looked just like him. Then, as she blinked in confusion and tried again, she managed to reduce the crowd to one leaning figure.

"What'm I doin' . . ." Her words were so garbled that she had to swallow and start over. "What am I doing here?"

"Recovering from your hangover," was his terse reply.

"That may take years." She put a hand to the top of her head to discover an ice bag and pulled it off to stare at its familiar shape.

"You've only been out about three hours," Kent told her with unfeeling logic. "The doc said you'd be sitting up and wanting dinner in four."

"Dinner?" Barbara repeated the word with loathing. "No way. All I want now is a glass of water." She decided that she could make it to the bathroom under her own steam and pushed back the blanket covering her before swinging her feet to the floor. As she took her first lurching steps, it occurred to her that she was wearing pajamas which were familiar and a robe which wasn't. Her head came up at that and she fixed Kent with an accusing, bleary gaze. "How did I get in this?"

"Don't blame me," he said hastily. "I keep

telling you that I'm just an innocent bystander. A policewoman brought you here and undressed you, along with the doctor I called in. A woman doctor who came highly recommended," he added virtuously. "She said you don't have to worry about any lasting effects. A Mickey Finn hasn't killed anybody yet."

"Your sympathy overwhelms me," Barbara told him as she started toward the bathroom door again. Her exit line would have been more effective if she'd managed to find the doorknob at first go, but that was difficult when she appeared to have a choice of two.

She felt a little better when she emerged. By then, she'd washed her face and combed her hair in between drinking three glasses of water. That didn't do anything to assuage her headache, but it did improve her outlook on life.

Kent was waiting for her in the foyer and took her in a firm grip to steer her back to the living room couch. "Let's try it as a crow flies this time instead of the Great Circle Route," he said, helping her across the room. When he'd made sure she was comfortable and sitting up against the bolster with a blanket across her legs, he said, "How about some tea?"

"I really don't want . . ."

"The British claim it's good for everything— even better than chicken soup," he continued as if she hadn't opened her mouth. "Besides, we don't have any chicken soup. I haven't had time to go shopping."

"I thought you were going to claim that the roofers finished it for lunch," she said, giving him a speaking glance.

"The roofers? Oh—yes."

As the awkward silence lengthened, she said with satisfaction, "You lied in your teeth."

"Well . . ."

"Again," she finished implacably.

"I'll get the tea."

She noted that his exit into the kitchen was more in the nature of a rout than anything else and she sank back on her pillows contentedly. As long as she was suffering, she decided, it was a pity not to share the wealth. It seemed safe enough; Kent wouldn't have hung around the flat waiting for her to surface unless he cared a little bit about her well-being.

That surge of hope made her wait expectantly for his reappearance. When he came back bearing a steaming mug of tea, she took it from him without any further objections.

"I hope that helps," he said, obviously trying to brace her up.

"It would take a gallon to have any effect." She watched him go back to the kitchen and emerge with a mug of his own. "What are you having?"

"Coffee laced with brandy." Before she could object, he pointed out, "I don't have a hangover. This"—he waved the mug in her direction as he sat down on the opposite sofa—"is purely medicinal to settle my shattered nerves. And if I stick around you much longer, I'll need something stronger."

She sat up indignantly, almost spilling her tea in the process. "I do *not* make a habit of hangovers."

"Well, if you will lark around with your seedy friends," he began and then broke off in alarm. "For God's sake, don't throw that! It's *Capo di Monte* and I'd be bankrupted trying to replace it for Philip."

"Oh, Lord, you mean it's an original? And I've been using it for the cocktail crackers." Barbara replaced the ornate porcelain dish on the table with exaggerated care before fixing him with a distracted glance. "That's just like everything else where you're concerned—it's one big secret."

"You didn't give me much of a chance to bare my soul," he reminded her, stretching out his long legs in front of him. "I'm not the only guilty one in that regard. Some women would have mentioned that they planned to jump ship in Norway instead of letting me find out about it afterwards from the purser."

His accusation made her head ache even harder for an instant and she made a palpable effort to subdue it by moving the ice bag around. "That's a low blow," she told him, after she had it balanced again. "You might have mentioned that you weren't going to the Shetlands."

"Where in the hell did you get that idea?"

She recoiled at his violent reply. "Well, that's

what Janice told Derek in the corridor outside my stateroom. She couldn't find you at the airport when she checked in for your flight."

"That was the aim of the game. I'd set up a charter, because I didn't want her along when I first met Philip. He'd had his suspicions about her lately, but God knows, we never thought she was fool enough to be in your friend Derek's pocket."

"He's *not* my friend—"

"I know that now," Kent cut in, "and I shouldn't give you a bad time about him after what happened at Chelsea, but it was a shock when you appeared with him in tow."

"You mean—you thought—" The idea was so ludicrous that she could only shake her head and then wince as she discovered that wasn't a good idea either.

"Well, look at it from the official point of view. There was all this speculation about that oil exploration report and the ministry knew that the investment capital would run to millions. That's why the security had to be so tight on the project. Philip wanted me to check out the final data as an impartial consultant—it was just another safeguard against slip-ups." Kent shifted on the couch, evidence that the small sofa wasn't designed for his six-foot frame.

Barbara pressed the ice bag even more tightly to her head, wondering if she'd heard correctly. "Maybe I'm still groggy," she said finally, "but I honestly don't see why he'd call you in—even if you are his stepson. What does a photographer know about oil exploration?"

"Well . . . to be honest . . ." Kent was obviously searching for the right words as he swirled the liquid in his mug.

"That would be a nice change," she murmured, watching him.

His glance came up quickly. "What do you mean?"

"Honesty," she said, ignoring his indignant response. "Was the photography angle another act?"

"Not at all," he replied in a smug tone. "I do take pictures and there will be a very nice calendar published, but . . ."

"Go ahead. Drop the other shoe."

"The photography's a hobby," he confessed. "I'm also a petroleum engineer. That's how I met Philip in the first place some years ago. Before he joined the government ministry, he came to Texas to consult with the people in our firm about a joint exploration venture. That's when he met my mother."

Barbara forgot all about her anger in the light of this newer, more fascinating disclosure. "Go on," she urged, when he paused.

"I'm going as fast as I can," he assured her with a crooked grin. "Anyhow, they hit it off right away, but she'd been a widow for ten years and it took some persuasion on Philip's part to make her remarry and cross the Atlantic with him. They were happy, though, until she died in an automobile accident here last year." At Barbara's instinctive murmur of distress, he nodded grimly. "A drunk driver came over the center line and she was killed instantly. Anyhow," he took a deep breath and went on, "Philip's been great. Couldn't have been nicer if I'd been his real son. That's why I try to come over whenever I have any time off. This trip was a combination of business and pleasure."

"Until I appeared on the scene," Barbara said, viewing it from a new angle.

"Right. You were the fly in the soup . . . so to speak," he said, his expression softening again. "Philip had been occupying the flat, but I arrived after he'd gone north to the Shetlands. It never occurred to us that Janice would take a tenant without checking first. That made it seem as if you'd been put on the scene deliberately—especially when Derek showed up on the doorstep."

"You'd heard of him?"

"There were rumors about his involvement in Mid-East affairs and I thought I recognized him after he talked to you that first day."

"Which made me seem even guiltier," she concluded.

"Something like that." Kent finished his coffee and put his empty mug on the table at his elbow. "The authorities decided to play along, but keep you under surveillance."

"Hence the modeling 'job' and a free cruise," she said with some bitterness. "How about your 'sprained' ankle?"

"That was pure coincidence, but it gave me

the perfect excuse to put you aboard ship. I hadn't planned on such realism," he admitted wryly.

"I see." Barbara leaned back against her pillow as she tried to think about all that had happened. "And that attack in Bergen?"

"Derek must have been getting a little desperate by then. He was a friend of Janice's ex-husband and I gather that he struck up a nice little affair with her to keep her handy. She claims he's a representative for a Middle-East syndicate, who instructed him to learn about the details on the newest exploration. When they didn't have any luck in London, Derek tried to buy some more time with the episode in Bergen. If we'd ended in the hospital as a result, it might have caused Philip some concern and delayed things a bit. After that tactic failed, Redmayne and Janice evidently decided to cover the action one on one; he'd follow you on the cruise ship, she'd try her seduction bit with me." When Barbara's eyes narrowed, he grinned and said, "They both struck out, so you can take that suspicious look off your face."

She ignored that to ask, "How did you find out about all this?"

"Janice." The amusement in his face disappeared at that disclosure. "After we nabbed Derek at the restaurant, she couldn't wait to tell us all she knew, in hopes of getting off lightly. She'd been warned earlier and advised to cooperate."

"Then you were there, after all?"

"At the flower show? Of course." He leaned forward, putting his elbows on his knees as he surveyed her. "But after you appeared with Derek, it seemed best to wait for a while. Then when we saw what had happened to you, the police staged that dodge of the clumsy waiter."

Anger rose in Barbara at his offhand comment. "So I was just an egg for your omelette—was that it? All the time I was wondering whether you were really all right or whether your stepfather was just leading me on." She shook her head despairingly. "I was even trying to hang onto that miserable caption book when Derek said it was what he'd been looking for all along."

"Hell's bells!" Kent said with a disgusted snort. "The information in that book wouldn't have done a thing for him. I certainly wouldn't have been fool enough to leave data worth millions of pounds in a woman's purse!"

"Thanks very much. It's nice to know exactly how I rate."

"I meant," he said with terrible patience, "that I'd put you in enough danger already—that's why I thought it was safer to leave you in Bergen. Although if it's any consolation to your pride, I'll admit that I forgot all about the damned book after I kissed you. I didn't even think about it again until I was halfway over the North Sea. When I contacted the purser aboard the ship, you'd already done a flit."

"So I wasn't the only one—" she murmured, so surprised that she wasn't aware of saying it aloud.

"Walking around in a fog after that kiss?" He stood up and strode restlessly to the other side of the room, as if putting a safer distance between them. "Hardly. My God! You should know by now that I'm lucky to even remember my name when you're within reach."

"I never would have known it," she breathed, still scarcely able to believe her ears. "Are you sure that *you* feel all right?"

"Oh, absolutely." His tone was cynical. "At least as good as any man could feel when he sees his girl lying unconscious after he's dragged her into a lousy mess. I should have sent you off to a hotel that first day you walked in but . . ."

When his jaw tightened and he didn't say anything more, Barbara beat both fists on the cushion in frustration. "Damn it all! Next you'll be apologizing again! I wish to heaven that for once you'd stop being so damned upstanding and stuffy—" She broke off in alarm as he came toward her like a tornado, gathering speed on the way.

"Stuffy, am I? That's all the thanks I get for trying to do something right for a change," he snarled as he yanked her roughly against him.

His kiss was devastating but punishing at the same time—as if he were trying to extract the last measure of revenge by invading her parted lips. Then, after an interminable moment, his mouth softened, but even before Barbara could respond, he'd pushed her at arm's length again and groaned, "Hell! I'm sorry—I must be losing my mind. I promised myself that I'd let you get well before I laid a finger on you and then look what happens." He stood up and went in the dressing room, emerging an instant later with his coat over his arm.

Barbara was still trying to get her breath, but that apology—when his last one at Bergen was still haunting her—was too much. "I don't know what you think is going to happen once I get rid of the headache," she flared back at him, "but I wouldn't count on any lasting relationship." Then she spoiled the whole ultimatum by asking, "Where are you going now?"

"To tell Philip that we won't be coming to see him tonight. After that, I'll see if I can scrounge a bed at his hotel, so you can relax for the rest of the night."

His proposed schedule didn't do a thing to improve her feelings. If anything, Barbara's headache seemed to get worse at the news. She clamped her lips together tightly to keep them from trembling and concentrated on adjusting her ice bag, as if that were her only concern.

"Want me to refill that for you before I leave?" he asked.

"No, thanks," she said, stopping him in his tracks. She took a deep breath then and announced in her coolest tones, "We really should settle who'll be keeping the flat for the rest of my stay in London."

"I'd sort of thought that problem would take care of itself—" he began quietly.

His hooded expression didn't alter as she stared back at him. There didn't seem to be much doubt that he wanted her—his actions had shown that—

but only as a temporary vacation companion. He'd
decided they could have a brief fling and afterward
go their separate ways with a few memories. Only
for her, the memories wouldn't compensate for
months of heartache and the knowledge that
wanting didn't mean the same thing as loving.

"If you meant that we'd share the flat," she
cut in, keeping her tone without expression as
she went on with scarcely a pause, "I don't really
think that would work. It's better if we finish
the whole thing now."

It was a terrible effort to get her last words
out, because at that moment what she truly
wanted was to have him take her in his arms
again. Only not just for a night, but a lifetime.

Kent opened his mouth as if to protest and
then his lips came together with a dreadful final-
ity. He gave her one last, long look before he
turned and slammed out the door.

Barbara didn't even try to stop the tears that
flooded her eyes and dripped onto her pale cheeks.
She got to her feet with painful determination
and headed for the kitchen. She'd refill the
damned ice bag and rest for a few more minutes—
then she'd pack her belongings and find a hotel
near the airport until she could get a flight home.

As she reached for the refrigerator door, her
glance was caught by a huge fragrant bouquet
at the other end of the counter. The glass vase
brimmed with bright yellow freesias and at the
base of it—next to a box of tea bags—there was
a leather ring box and some kind of legal docu-
ment.

She impatiently mopped her tears with one hand as she clutched the paper with the other. Her eyes skimmed the official phrases about a special license to wed before seeing her name listed with Kent's.

Barbara didn't wait any longer. She made a mad dash for the front door of the flat. Fortunately Kent stepped out of the elevator before she got halfway down the hall.

She threw herself into his willing arms, saying almost incoherently, "Darling! Why didn't you tell me? I thought you were planning an affair all along."

"Sssh! You'll shock the neighbors," he said, dropping a quick kiss on her wet cheek as he hustled her back in the flat and closed the door behind them. "So you *did* get the wrong idea. I thought you might have. That's why I came back." He pulled her close with such relief that she wondered how she could have ever gotten such an addlepated notion.

"Well, you didn't ever say anything about marriage," she said, burrowing into his shirt front, "and I knew I'd never survive any other kind of relationship with you. If you love someone—" her voice stumbled over the words before gathering strength. "I could never just walk away afterwards."

"The only time you'll have the chance is about sixty years from now," he said in a firm tone that put her last qualms to rest. "And you needn't think you have a monopoly on falling in love— I knew that I wanted to marry you about five minutes after you invaded the flat. But I still don't understand why you were running up and down the hall in my bathrobe. You're supposed to be in bed."

"I had to catch up with you," she confessed. "I'd just found the flowers and all the rest."

Her flushed cheeks at that confession made him grin and he flicked the end of her nose with a gentle finger. "In that case, go back in there and lie down. We'll find out if the ring fits and afterwards we'll check in with Philip. He's seeing if we can use that special marriage license tomorrow if he clears it with the Embassy." He frowned as he tried to concentrate, finding it hard with Barbara's delectable figure close in his arms. "I don't think I've forgotten anything," he said, his voice not as steady as it might have been.

"There are one or two items," she said in a provocative tone that brought his head down to survey her carefully.

"You're back to normal," he said with great satisfaction as he steered her toward the couch in the living room. "I have a couple of things in mind myself."

"And if you apologize again . . ."

Her threat didn't even get started before she was cut off in the nicest way possible and she shivered with pleasure as her body came alive under his exploring hands.

At his hotel some hours later, Sir Philip wasn't surprised that he hadn't heard from Kent or his daughter-in-law to be. He did hope, however, that they wouldn't be late for the ceremony in the morning. After all, it wasn't every day that a stepfather had a chance to arrange a wedding.

The most difficult part was deciding whether or not to have champagne for the reception—considering the recent circumstances. But Barbara seemed to be a sensible young woman as well as a beautiful one, so he'd gone ahead and ordered the finest vintage.

Sir Philip smiled at the thought of the pleasure in store for the future and he finally went to bed, reasoning sensibly that at least one of the bridal party should have a decent night's sleep.

About the Author

Glenna Finley is a native of Washington State. She earned her degree from Stanford University in Russian Studies and in Speech and Dramatic Arts, with emphasis on radio.

After a stint in radio and publicity work in Seattle, she went to New York City to work for NBC as a producer in its international division. In addition, she worked with the "March of Time" and *Life* magazine.

As a producer, she had her own show about activities in Manhattan, a show that was broadcast to England. The programs were similar to those of the "Voice of America."

Though her life in New York was exciting, she eventually returned to the Northwest where she married. Currently residing in Seattle with her husband, Donald Witte, and their son, she loves to travel, and draws heavily on her travels and experiences for the novels that have been published. Her books for NAL have sold several million copies.

𝕆

Romantic Fiction from SIGNET